AVENGE ME

Lisa Cindrich & Jay Sparks

UNMOORED
PRESS

Text copyright © 2016 Lisa Cindrich & James Sparks

Published by Unmoored Press 2016

www.unmooredpress.com

ISBN 978-0-9982431-0-8 (paperback)

.

TABLE OF CONTENTS

FIRST KILL..7
SOUL SAVER OF SOLEDAD...35
AVENGE ME...72
WHATEVER IT TAKES...100
CLAY..125
RAYFID & BIDDY...163
EMERALD CITY...193

FIRST KILL

TOMMY HAD NEVER HUNTED a human before, but he knew he'd be good at it. All he'd ever needed was a chance, and Uncle Merle was finally giving him that. Sure, the job was low-level, bottom rung of the ladder at Uncle Merle's execution company, but Tommy didn't care. It was a start. First step toward some kind of future that didn't involve shoving stock around a big box store between midnight and eight a.m., three nights a week. Toward a career—yeah, a career, a *profession*—that would sling him right at the bullseye: money, excitement, coworkers who didn't grime up his ears with a lot of stupid whining or grime up his lungs with the weed they smoked on the loading dock.

And if Uncle Merle hired him on full-time, Tommy would be on the road. A lot. Away from Crystal.

Major plus.

He powered his pickup along the driveway and cut the motor in front of the small ranch house they rented from Crystal's mother. Crystal's mom had waived the first month's rent and called that a wedding gift, but she'd still scraped a look up and down Tommy, announced "I don't trust him not to trash the place," and shoved her hand out for the security deposit. The rent was cheap, but the house was a piece of crap: a leaky roof, the porch rotting away at one end, a downspout fallen across the shriveled grass like some skinwaste overdosing in the yard.

It was late afternoon and sultry, the air motionless. The truck's A/C was busted, but he'd be getting that fixed as soon as he bagged his first kill and got that first bonus. Sweat soaked through the back of his shirt. He glanced in the rearview mirror, rubbed a hand across his brush cut and admired its military efficiency. Goddamn, but he looked tough. His cheekbones were hard and his jaw squared when he clenched it.

He looked like a hitter. Like the next Mike Renz.

Pulling his shoulders back, he stepped through the front door. He'd played defense on his high school football team, varsity all but his freshman year, his solid six-foot-two build giving him an immediate advantage over the scrawnier guys. He'd plumped for quarterback—could've drilled the ball to the receivers if he'd just had a chance—but Coach hadn't liked him and never gave him the nod. The principal's kid got quarterback. Big surprise.

The living room was small and dark. Depressing as hell, especially for somebody like him, an outdoor kind of guy. Crystal had bought the couch and coffee table at a garage sale. Both pieces were a murky black-brown, cockroach-colored and about as attractive. A pillow angled strategically against the back of the couch couldn't conceal an ever-lengthening gash in the upholstery. Water rings overlapped one another, all the way up and down the coffee table.

Nothing like Mike Renz's condo. Tommy had been there once. Not actually been there, but watched a holo Uncle Merle had recorded of a meeting in Renz's living room. The place was all bright white walls, glass and chrome furniture, windows that rose floor to ceiling, the green leaves of sycamores shimmering and flashing outside. Hardwood floors gleaming like oil. No wife to gunk up the works. Who needed a wife if you could afford maid service?

Tommy paused, pulled out his comm, and logged into their bank account. He'd been checking it reflexively every few minutes. The credit statement always posted on the first of the month. If he could get it paid—well, get the minimum paid—so the statement automatically migrated over to the 'transaction completed' sector, Crystal might not even notice it.

He worked his jaw muscles. Crystal? Not notice a bill? Hell, the woman crawled all over those things, like a fly on dog shit. The fresher the bill, the faster she was on it.

Sure enough. Tommy squinted at the comm. The bill had posted eight minutes ago, while he was occupied driving the truck, and had already been viewed. Not paid. Viewed.

His fingers cramped around the comm. A familiar sick sensation slid through his belly, his body preparing itself for the onslaught of complaints and eye-rolling.

But then he remembered the job Uncle Merle was going to give him. The bonus. Crystal had nothing to hang over him now.

The hallway was skinny and short as a closet. The kitchen was at its other end and he could hear them back there. A pan rang against the range top. Water pounded the sink. Darrell was pretending to shoot something, shrilling "bang!" and "ka-POW!" every other second.

One step into the kitchen and Darrell plunged at him. The boy waved a toy machine gun in one hand and brandished a cherry popsicle in the other. Sticky red juice trailed down his snub chin like a bloody beard. The toy gun clattered to the floor. Darrell grabbed at Tommy's leg and clung there like a bramble.

Tommy ran a rough hand across the boy's head. "Okay," he said. "Okay. Jesus." He gave Darrell a swat and kicked the fallen gun toward the boy. "Guess you liked your birthday present, yeah?" He threw a glance toward Crystal. She stood at the sink, her back to the room.

"Watch this, Daddy!" Snatching up the toy, Darrell aimed for the refrigerator. "Pow!" He looked back at Tommy, face alight, waiting for praise.

Tommy put out a hand, pretended to stagger when Darrell smashed a palm against it and shouted, "High five!"

Tommy glanced over at his wife's back again. She wore jeans and a faded blue t-shirt, the cotton thin enough to show every clip and fastener of the bra beneath it. "Solid hit, huh, Crystal? He's a natural. That fridge isn't going anywhere anytime soon."

Crystal shoved back the handle on the faucet. The water diminished to a steady trickle that didn't stop. She shook her hands, flinging water drops against the stained porcelain. Turning, she leaned back against the edge of the countertop and folded her arms. Her damp hands glimmered.

"You said last week you were going to fix this sink," she said and sharpened her stare on Tommy as if he were a whetstone.

"I'm getting to it," Tommy answered before he even thought to stop himself. He had the damn job from Uncle Merle practically jammed in his back pocket. He didn't have to bow down to anybody. He re-squared his shoulders, jutted his chin.

Darrell held the miniature gun sight up to one eye and aimed at his mother's leg. "Bang! Got you!"

Squirreling up her mouth, Crystal pushed the gun barrel away. Her eyes never shifted from Tommy. "So? When you planning to get to it?"

"Daddy! Was it a good shot?"

Tommy gave the boy a good-natured swat. "Sure it was. But remember what I told you? Dad. Not Daddy."

Darrell took off, sprinting toward the miniscule backyard, banging the screen door aside, gun jabbing this way and that like the stinger of a crazed wasp.

"So?" Crystal's gaze pinned him. "When?"

Hadn't her face been soft once? Since their marriage, right out of high school, her bones had turned into knife-edges and her cheeks had gone flat. Even her lips had narrowed and thinned though Tommy was damned if he understood how that could happen to a woman in just six years.

"Well, Crystal," he said, "I'm not sure just when I'll get around to that."

"Oh, that's great—" she started, her mouth wrinkling like the butt end of a pumpkin.

"I'm going to be pretty busy." Tommy shrugged, looked deliberately casual. Like Mike Renz, yeah, like Renz skimming over the specs for yet another hit to add to the long list of hits already in the bag.

"Actually," he announced, "Uncle Merle's got a job for me."

Crystal's mouth fell open. Tommy hooked a chair out from beneath the kitchen table and lounged down onto it. Yeah, this was what it felt like to be Renz. Strong. Electric. Like wires had replaced his veins and arteries and they were alive and snapping for action. He could do anything, absolutely anything. Kill with a touch. No Executable would stand a chance.

Crystal said, "You're kidding."

Tommy's hands became fists jammed against the tabletop. "No. I'm not kidding. Do I look like I'm—"

Crystal glanced out the back door. "Darrell! Stay out of those bushes! I told you there's poison ivy!" She looked at Tommy. "Since no one's dug that poison ivy out of there yet."

"Did you hear what I said?" Tommy asked.

"Yeah, I heard." Crystal scuffed across the floor. The tiles were sticky with popsicle drippings. She stabbed her skinny body down on another chair and crossed her legs, the top leg flicking back and forth. Dark grime clung to the sole of her foot. No pretty pink-painted nails, not since high school. "I heard you, but the thing is, I don't know that I believe you."

"It's sure great to have a wife who supports me."

"Damn right," Crystal answered. "I support you and Darrell and this whole place."

"What? I have a job."

"You call that a job? While I'm doing 40-plus at Food Savers, plus the temping? I haven't seen you even try to get any construction work lately."

The skin across Tommy's knuckles strained, white streaks marbling the flesh. "Construction's seasonal. You know that."

"Yeah, well, 'tis the season right now."

"Harry's laying off this year. Not hiring."

Crystal leaned forward. Tommy smelled potato chips on her breath. She was always filling her body with garbage. "We aren't going to make the next rent."

Tommy had to fight the urge to squirm. Like he was a dumb kid and she was a teacher. It was ridiculous, especially when he was on the verge of finally making some real money.

He shifted his butt on the chair and heard himself say, "We're good. We've got, what a couple weeks?"

"You don't even know what day it's due. The fourth. Every month. The fourth. Except this month we can't pay half of it." She tugged her comm out of the back pocket of her jeans. "And looky what's been going on the credit card." Tommy could make out enough of the screen to see their bank's logo at the top. Crystal frowned at the comm. "How many times can a man go to Guns Blazing in one month anyway?" she asked.

"I needed ammo."

Crystal tapped her finger down the screen. "Six times?"

"I've gotta keep the skills sharp. Especially now." Tommy interlaced his fingers, elaborately cracked his knuckles. Thought *Renz would never do that* and dropped his hands to the table again.

"Because your uncle's about to let you tag along on a hit."

"*Do* the hit."

Crystal shoved the comm back in her pocket. "So what's the job?"

"I don't have the exact—"

"I knew you were full of shit."

"I've got an appointment with him."

"When?" she asked.

"Tomorrow."

"What time?"

"Jesus!" Tommy exploded up from his seat. "Look. I happen to know Uncle Merle's having big problems with some of his hitters. He can't give every job to—to Mike Renz or Chistyakov or Eisen or—" Tommy's mind, white with fury, went blank. "—those caliber guys. Uncle Merle's looking for new blood, okay? He needs real marksmen. He needs me."

He pressed toward his wife, looming over her, silently daring her to attack him. Instead, she let out a long breath.

"I wish it would happen," she said. Her voice was suddenly as slumped and listless as her posture. "I wish you could make something out of all those toys you buy, the guns, the bow hunting crap." Crystal's eyes were rimmed rabbit-pink. She had allergies from March clear through November. "That we had some money. I wish—"

Shaking her head, she stood and stepped across to the sink. She turned on the hot water, picked up a dirty plate, then just stood there, motionless, her back to

Tommy and steam ribboning toward her face. Stray tendrils of hair that had escaped her ponytail wisped soft and damp against her neck.

Back after high school, when they first got married, she'd always worn her long hair caught up in some sort of clasp and Tommy had loved to finger the loose bits around her face. He hadn't been able to stop himself from touching her hair, not back then, or from stroking her neck. She'd aged fifteen years in the last six, but her neck was still bird-slender, her hair the same rich walnut.

He reached for her now, his hand just floating above the nape of her neck. "I've got the job, baby."

Crystal stiffened. She snapped on a pair of rubber gloves and started scrubbing the plate. "I'll believe that when I see the money." She didn't look back at him. "Go check on Darrell, will you? Make sure he's not in that poison ivy."

Tommy jerked away. "You check on him. I'm busy." He strode across the kitchen and had just reached the tiny hallway when his comm buzzed. He snatched at it, stopped dead when he saw the ID. For a second, he didn't think he could answer it. His pulse drummed against his jawbone and hammered his wrists like somebody had just turned up the volume on his heart.

The comm kept buzzing. Crystal swung around from the sink. "Could you answer that thing already?" Then she saw his face and shut up. Stood there watching him, her hands dripping onto the floor. "It's him?"

Tommy stared back at her, nodded. "I—yeah. Give me a second here." He hunched into the living room, stood at the picture window while gathering his courage. The front yard was a simmering blur of browns and greens under a smear of blue sky.

He thumbed the comm. "Tom here. Oh, hey, Uncle Merle. How you doing?"

Crystal appeared in the hallway. Her stare burned. He shouldered away from her, flicked the comm to audio only-private. No need to let her in on the conversation, not if there was any chance Uncle Merle was about to tell him he wasn't good enough to join Renz and the company's other killers.

Not that Uncle Merle was going to say that.

And he didn't.

∞

Five minutes later, Tommy was pushing the comm down in his pocket and treating his wife to a look of complete, Renz-like nonchalance. It was hard to keep himself in a relaxed pose, not a care in the world, when he really wanted to fling himself around like Darrell on a sugar rush. He wanted to bound up on the ugly coffee table, stamp on it, trampoline on the ugly couch. Tear that stuffing out with his boot heels. He could buy a better couch when he got his bonus.

"What?" he asked Crystal. Turned his palms up like he didn't understand what she wanted to know. "That was just Uncle Merle. Giving me the job. Like I told you." Now a grin cracked his face. He couldn't stop it. "I got to be in New Mexico Friday. The Executable's supposed to be walking out of Toluca prison at oh-seven-thirty Saturday morning. And I'll be right there, waiting with a bullet. It's only gonna take one."

Crystal looked dumbfounded. Tommy's grin was an assault rifle. Thought he was a screw up? Well, let her stew in her apologies. He'd forgive her . . . eventually.

"I need to get ready," he said. "Get a few supplies." He strutted to the front door. It felt good just to be in motion. It would feel even better to be at the store. He had to ditch these old t-shirts. Buy some of those white shirts like Renz wore, rugged outdoor kind of stuff. Really made a tan stand out. Made the shoulders look big and square. "Bonus'll be in the bank by next week."

Crystal just kept watching him.

"What?" he snapped.

"Just . . . please." Those dark eyes on him, not angry but something worse.   Jaded. Skeptical. "Please, Tommy. Don't screw this one up."

∞

Toluca Penitentiary—a collection of ugly, burnt-gray buildings encompassed by layers of vicious-looking fencing—squatted in the scrubby New Mexico desert seven miles from the nearest town. The town of the same name was also ugly and squat, hunkered in on itself, each flat roof and dilapidated car radiating hostility: Go away.

Tommy paced a narrow strip of parking lot outside his motel room. His gear was in the car, ready to head out for the job. "Time," he said.

"Oh-four-thirty," responded his comm, the sound muffled by his shirt pocket. The voice was female and friendly, the accent Aussie. The kind of woman he should have married.

He stopped in front of 122, the room adjacent to his own. Heavy curtains covered the front window. He couldn't tell if there was a light on inside.

"Time," he repeated.

"Oh-four-thirty two."

He looked east. The sky was still dark. Sunrise wasn't till 5:52. He'd checked that in the days leading up to the trip. Checked it several times.

He turned back to 122's door. Under artificial lights, its red paint had an orange tint like old blood. Shadows of moths ricocheted across the surface like random bullets.

They had to get going. They'd agreed on 0430. If Sergei Chistyakov wasn't ready—was still asleep, maybe? Jesus. Then it was up to Tommy to keep this job on track.

He wished for about the thousandth time that he'd pulled Renz as his partner. Sergei was one of the big guys in Regency Execution Inc.'s stable, but he had a reputation as a wild card. Got the job done every time, but with a certain amount of drama. Unpredictability. Or as Crystal put it: cruelty. Which was typical of her, ignorant about hitters and what they did, but never failing to shoot off her mouth like she knew everything.

How many times did Tommy have to explain it to her? "These Executables are scum of the earth," he'd told her, repeating what he'd heard Uncle Merle proclaim a hundred times at wedding receptions and family reunions. "Murderers, rapists. If their victims' families want some final justice served up with a little 'cruelty,' so what? It's all legal and it's their right. And they're willing to pay for it. So why don't you just shut your mouth?"

Still, word was Renz was every bit as effective as Sergei, but methodical. Worked in a way that would make it easy for a new guy like Tommy to learn the regs, learn the ropes. Renz did the jobs without any extra flourish or extra blood. Just got 'em done and got out.

Got the bonus.

Okay, Sergei was now officially five minutes late. Time to step up. Tommy balled up a fist and knocked. Made it loud and strong.

The door popped open.

Sergei bounded out of the darkness, a zippered canvas bag swinging from one hand, a rifle case from the other. "Good morning! It is a good morning? Very exciting for you, yes."

Tommy stepped back, startled. "Uh—"

Sergei popped the trunk, tossed the bag and rifle case inside, slammed the lid. He stretched an arm out to each side, threw back his head, and took a deep breath that pushed out his square chest. The Russian was barely five-and-a-half feet tall, but muscular. Thick brown hair coated his bare arms and burst from under his collar to shadow the lower third of his neck. He radiated rude vigor and strength.

"You are feeling ready?" Sergei asked.

Keep it cool, keep it old-hand-at-killing. "Oh, yeah." Tommy flicked a hand toward the car. "I've got all my stuff in there too. Just waiting for us hitters to do our thing."

"Us hitters?" Sergei pressed close. A sauerkraut odor hung from his mouth.

Tommy's mouth flinched into a shit-eating grin before he could stop himself. "Yeah, I mean...it's just my first job, I know that, but I'm on Unc—I'm on

Regency's payroll now. Official." His shoulders rose, dropped. "Right?"

Sergei clapped him on the back so hard that Tommy's teeth clicked together. "Not right. No. You? A hitter? No."

Tommy stared, face suddenly hot. Sergei practically bounded past him, hoisted the driver's-side door open, and popped behind the wheel.

Stand up for yourself! Don't let him talk to you like that.

Tommy swung himself between the seat and the door before Sergei could pull it shut. "I'm on the hit. So what do you think that makes me?"

The Russian fixed a stare on him that snagged Tommy like a fishhook through skin. "So. You are on your first job. I am on my—" Sergei briefly raised his fingers from the steering wheel, but his eyes didn't move. "One hundred fifty-eighth, yes. But of course, you are right. We are hitters, yes? Both of us. Equal."

Tommy shifted his weight. Sweat dribbled from his armpits, turning the fabric of his white, Renz-style shirt clammy and dark. "Look, I'm not trying to say I've got your kind of experience, or anyth—hey!"

Sergei bounced up from his seat and stood aside, gesturing Tommy to take his place. "Please. Yes. You sit there." Sergei fluttered his fingers toward the empty seat. "You."

Tommy peered at the Russian. "I don't really care who drives and who—"

"Sit."

Tommy sank onto the seat.

Sergei leaned in. Tommy unobtrusively sipped the pungent sauerkraut air through his mouth. "You are now the number one hitter on this job," Sergei told him. "You understand that?"

"Uh, my unc—I mean, according to what Regency told me, we're both assigned this hit."

"I want to show you my feelings of—what?—sorry. I gave you an insult."

"It's okay, man, I don't—"

"I make it right. You do this job. You do the hit."

A slow panic crawled up from the pit of Tommy's belly. "What about you?"

"I will be what you call just back-up. Boring, yes? I sit back. I watch."

"Watch me do the whole thing? Set up and kill the guy?"

"You are so good, maybe I learn some tricks from you."

"But I thought—Uncle Mer—I mean, the boss said you'd be, like, mentoring me."

Sergei flicked the notion away like a speck of dirt. "He says that every time there is a first hit. His little joke, yes? Because really? This is more a—what do you call it? A sink or swim kind of a thing."

Tommy swallowed past what seemed to be a sudden, massive tumor in his throat. "Oh. Okay." What the hell else could he say?

Sergei trotted around to the other side of the car and flung himself into the passenger seat. "Good," he said. "Now, you drive."

∞

The desert surrounding Toluca Penitentiary was a perfect killing field. Flat. Barren apart from an occasional scraggly shrub or low cactus. Ancient telephone poles stabbed up at haphazard angles from the cracked dirt. Dawn vomited orange and pink over the horizon.

Tommy slid out of his seat. His comm buzzed at him. He snatched at it. *Uncle Merle.*

Instead, Crystal's head bulged up, lemon-sour, from the device. It was going on oh-eight-thirty back on the east coast and, judging from her pouchy eyes and the tuft of hair sprouting, Alfalfa-style, from the clip at the back of her head, she obviously hadn't gotten any beauty sleep. The woman was an insomniac anyway, rustling and slithering all over her half of the bed, making sure that if she couldn't sleep, neither could Tommy.

Tommy rabbited around to the trunk and hunched over the comm like he was trying to keep a match lit in a strong wind. "What?" he said. "I'm kind of busy here."

"My mom just called."

Tommy peered over his shoulder. Shit. Sergei's door flung open. The Russian sprang out and stretched, rising onto his toes.

Tommy pushed his mouth right up to the holo like he was trying to kiss his wife. "I'm in the middle of a hit."

Crystal ignored that. "I couldn't pay the rent."

"So it's one day overdue. She's not gonna—"

He paused, staring at Sergei who dropped to the desert floor to reel out an easy dozen pushups, then hopped back up and settled against the trunk. Tommy shifted in a half-circle, trying to keep his back to Sergei and the holo concealed.

"She's got to give us a couple days. A—a—" What the hell did they call it? "Grace period. Yeah. So will you stop worrying about it and give me some air here? Let me do my job. Uncle Merle'll probably have the bonus in our account today."

Sergei leaned in, leering at Crystal. "Not today, no. Before the bonus, you must wait for the, ah, the verification. Yes? Paperwork. Always the paperwork." He raised his shoulders and hands in grinning exasperation

Tommy shuffled a half-dozen feet away. "Just tell your mom to hang tight, will you? I'm busy here, okay?"

"She's in the driveway with a truck and that guy she's dating."

"What the hell are you even talking about?"

"They're moving my stuff and Darrell's over to her basement."

Images flashed into Tommy's head: his almost-new KL-65 rifle, his collection of hand guns, snares, camo, nunchucks, hunting bows. "What about my stuff?"

"Landfill."

Tommy twisted to look at the sunrise. The metal of the penitentiary fence glowed with an amber light. "Aww, shit, you mean right now?'

"Don't you want to ask where me and Darrell are going?"

That KL-65 wasn't even paid off yet. It was the deluxe model too.

An odor of sauerkraut wilted the morning breeze. Sergei's hand sliced the air between Tommy and the holo of Crystal. "Lover boy has work to do," the Russian sang, took the comm, and closed the connection.

"You take calls while you do a hit?" Sergei said. He clicked his tongue. "You make me start to think maybe you and me, maybe we are not so much equals."

Tommy held himself rigid and stared at the tips of his boots. His tongue twisted and pushed against the roof of his mouth, forming silent words. He wanted to explain about his wife, how she hadn't always been a bitch, how Tommy wouldn't have picked up the call if he'd realized it was her. But Sergei didn't seem like the kind of guy who'd want to listen to anybody's problems. Probably wasn't even married. No wedding ring, anyway.

"Here." Sergei held the comm out on his extended palm like he was offering a reward to a pet dog. Tommy took it, jammed it in a cargo pocket.

Sergei lounged against the car and didn't speak, just watched Tommy gather gear from the trunk. Tommy flicked glances at the man. Was he serious about the whole not-helping bit? He was going to let Tommy sink or swim on his own? The fucker was grinning up at the sky, not saying a word.

Thanks for nothing, shit-head. Well, Uncle Merle thought Tommy was ready. And Tommy knew he was ready. So to hell with Sergei. To hell with Crystal too, all her *Please don't screw this one up* b.s. He had nothing to worry about. Fish in a barrel, Uncle Merle called it. He said he always made sure he gave a hitter an easy job the first time around. Ease them into the process.

Tommy slung his gear onto his back and checked his comm. Okay. According to regs he had to position himself at least 300 yards off prison grounds. So 300 yards past the fence? Where was the release door? He zoomed the holo and squinted, turning the three-dimensional image so he could inspect all sides. The main entrance was obvious, as were the loading dock doors at the back where the barrels of industrial cleaners produced by the prison's factory line were shipped out and the raw ingredients sent in.

Tommy double and triple-checked the schematics. He hadn't been mistaken. There was no notation indicating exactly where the Executable would be coming from.

"Great," he muttered.

They wouldn't send the guy right out the front entrance, would they? Usually the poor saps got shoved out a back door somewhere and herded, if necessary, off prison grounds, right toward the hitter, waiting with finger steady on the trigger. So that meant the loading dock area at the back of the complex.

"And what is so great?" Sergei's voice boomed, practically in his ear. Tommy jerked, made a quick grab to catch his comm.

Jesus. The Russian was away from the car and planted just a couple feet from him.

Sergei scrutinized Tommy and grinned. "There is a problem maybe?"

Tommy snorted. "I can handle it." He punched some measurements into the GPS and started walking. Grit and rock crunched under the soles of his boots.

"Why you go that direction?" Sergei called after him.

Tommy paced out a few more feet. Stopped. Doubt quivered gently in his gut, like morning dew on grass. He didn't want to so much as glance back at Sergei, but couldn't seem to stop himself.

"They'll let him out at the back," Tommy finally said. "I'm staking out my position."

Sergei wagged his head, his forehead puckered with elaborate concern. "You saw this on the specs?"

"Uh, not exactly."

"Because I did not see that."

Tommy swung full around. His rifle clattered against his shoulder blades. "What, you mean you actually looked at it? I thought this whole hit was my deal."

Sergei grappled a hand at his own chest, like he'd taken a blow to his heart. "Of course I look. I am a professional. I earn my fifty-fifty of the bonus."

"Fifty-fifty?" Tommy stalked back toward Sergei. "Are you kidding me? You just said you're gonna sit back, put the whole job on me. What the fuck are you doing to earn any bonus?"

"Tommy, Tommy."

"Thomas."

"Oh, Tommy." Sergei strode to him, smacked a palm onto his shoulder. "I am here to keep you from the mistakes. Big responsibility, yes? If that Executable, he gets away? You think you get even one more chance from your uncle? From anybody? No."

The Russian's palm burned through Tommy's shirt. Fingers dug painfully into muscle. "The specs, they do not say where they release this man from, right?"

The fingers tightened, like they yearned to separate tendon and ligament from bone. Tommy winced. "Right. So I figured—"

"No, no, no." Sergei released his grip. Tommy fought the urge to massage his shoulder. "When the specs do not say, you assume the Executable comes from the front, okay? The main door." His smile showed teeth the same dirty yellow-brown color as the ground.

"Unc—Merle didn't tell me that."

Sergei's grin broadened. "Because he knew I would tell you."

Tommy stared. Heat crept like a rash past the collar of his shirt and up his throat. "But you said I was on my own. The hit was all mine."

"A hitter—a real one, I mean—asks any questions, asks any person. He makes sure he *knows*, yes? Knows what he has to know."

"That's not fair! You said—"

"To have the facts, yes, the facts that you need, that is the thing. Mike Renz, he would have not been afraid to ask me."

"I wasn't afraid," Tommy muttered, dribbling the words in the direction of his chest. Then, determined to prove it, he swung his head up, caught Sergei's eyes, and said, "So what makes you so sure you know the right door?"

"The specs—"

Tommy brayed above Sergei's voice. "The specs don't prove anything either way."

"Also, I have killed seven Executables right in this place. So that is some experience to listen to, yes?"

Tommy was silent.

Sergei smacked him on the back. "It is okay. But I think now the cut goes sixty-forty. Sixty for me."

Tommy's mouth worked, but before he could figure out how to protest, Sergei gave him an elaborate, silent-movie wink and said, "I kid you, I kid you. A joke!" Sergei pulled out his own comm and stabbed a finger at the screen. "You are tracking how the time goes, yes?"

Heart suddenly pumping, Tommy tore his comm from its pocket and spoke a quick time-check. After seven? Shit! How had it gotten so late? The sun was up, the dawn colors eaten away by the sky's brilliant, unbroken blue. He could practically feel the seconds falling through the air, colliding and ricocheting away.

"You see, you must never take a call from a woman," Sergei said. "Not while you work. Not if you want to work even one more time. Women." His eyebrows shrugged. "Pesty. Like flies. Mosquitoes."

Tommy was in motion. He'd never finished figuring the correct distance from the prison grounds. This hit had to be by the book, not a regulation even slightly nicked. Stretching the rules was for the big boys who'd proved their value to the company. Someday that would be him—*if you don't screw up* came the thought which he immediately hurled away—but not here, not today.

With his GPS, he tracked to the mandated distance, shrugged off his rifle and pack, and kneeled down to check his ammo.

It was then he noticed Sergei receding toward the fence.

Tommy jolted to his feet. "Hey!"

Sergei turned, waved.

"Hey! Where are you going?"

Sergei tapped the barrel of the rifle he held loosely with both hands across the front of his body. There was something strange about the rifle. It looked too thick, too heavy. "I am back-up," Sergei called out. "Remember?"

A buzzing vibrated around the perimeter of Tommy's brain. Time was moving too fast. He could *feel* the seconds and parts-of-seconds buzzing at him, humming away. His heart thrummed with a relentless insect rhythm.

"Well—wait—so aren't you gonna back up my shot?"

Sergei shook his head. "I make sure no one slips through."

"Slips through where?"

A shrug. "The sides. The back." Sergei turned and continued to follow the curve of the fence toward the rear of the facility.

"Hey!" Tommy shouted. "Hey!"

But Sergei didn't look back again.

The sides? The back? What the fuck was that when they knew the Executable was coming out the front?

Time-check. Less than ten. Tommy pulled a sniper's tripod out of his pack, snapped the legs straight, and positioned his rifle in the channel. If Sergei had stuck around to watch, Tommy would have been too embarrassed to use a crutch like this. It almost made him glad Sergei had rounded the back of the prison and was now out of sight. Tommy's gut was rumbling, his bladder was tight, sweat drooled from his forehead into his eyes, and suddenly he wasn't sure he could hit a stationary target at ten yards, much less a moving one at 300.

"It's okay. You're okay." He forced himself to breathe long and slow, settled into final position. Time to spare. He could do this.

The seconds clicked past.

Tommy never looked away from the entrance. The doors didn't move. The fence gates stared out stolidly like they hadn't budged in years and never would again. Tommy's right foot fidgeted, tapping out spastic rhythms against the ground. From what he'd heard, Executable releases usually went like clockwork, everything timed right down to the minute like some kind of NASA launch back when NASA used to launch things.

By the time another five minutes passed, his heart was lunging so hard in his chest that it ached. His comm buzzed. He snatched at it, but this time double-checked the ID. Sergei was right about that anyway— no way Tommy was going to let Crystal buzz in like a mosquito and distract him. Let her move out, whatever. She'd be sorry when he was one of the big hitters.

But this time it *was* Uncle Merle. Tommy sucked in a deep breath and decided to open audio only.

"Hey. You got things about wrapped up?" Uncle Merle asked.

"Uh—"

"I don't like waiting for my people to report in."

Tommy's throat felt like its own version of Death Valley: dry and dead. "Yeah, they were a couple minutes late with the release."

"That's pretty atypical."

"Well, that's how it went down."

"You want to give me a visual on the body?" There were luxurious creaking sounds like Uncle Merle was shifting around in his big leather chair. "The client's pretty eager for a look."

Tommy stared at the comm. He stared at the closed gates, the shut doors, the blank sandy ground stretching between him and the fence. There was nothing he could even pretend was a corpse collapsed off at a distance. The buzzing in his head was like a swarm. Too loud to think. He pictured Crystal's withering look, Uncle Merle shaking his head and telling him, "Sorry, son, you're going to have to re-think this whole hitter thing." Mike Renz and the other hot shots chewing on Tommy's colossal fuck-up, laughing.

He shut the audio channel. Tossed the comm in his pack like he'd never touch it again. He didn't know what he'd tell his uncle.

It was then that he noticed the smoke ribboning up past the prison roof. It was pale gray and came from behind the complex. It could have been trash burning, or had something to do with the factory contained within the penitentiary. But somehow he knew: It was the Executable.

He was already running as he threw the rifle across his back. He left his pack and the tripod in the dirt and sprinted as hard as he could along the fence line, following it around to the back of the compound.

A sickly smell of partially roasted meat surged on the breeze. Tommy slowed, stumbled forward. A body smoldered twenty yards ahead. One arm gleamed pinkly in the sunlight; the rest of the body was a black carcass.

Sergei stood above it. His legs were spread in a solid victory stance. When he saw Tommy, he flung a smile, raised his rifle overhead with both arms straight, shook it and whooped.

No, Tommy thought, not a rifle. Some sort of modified hybrid rifle-flamethrower. Because this was Sergei and every damn story Tommy had heard about

Sergei seemed to involve fire or explosives or pincers or thumbscrews or electrical current.

The Russian's smile sliced like a knife in the gut.

Tommy couldn't move, just stared at the grinning hitter and the charred Executable. "You were supposed to be my back-up," Tommy said.

"And good thing I was, yes?" Sergei prodded a chunk of flaky flesh with one boot. "Or this thing, it would have run right out of here and free."

"You said he was coming out the front. You told me that."

"Oh, Tommy. A real hitter? He never takes a word for something. Not till he can say, yes! I know I can trust that man! This is a lesson for you, yes? I am, I think, a good teacher." He dangled the weapon. "You comm Merle now. Show him the body. Tell him this was all you."

"Lie to him?"

"I will back you up."

Tommy's hands clenched. He swarmed forward, fists pumping, but Sergei already had pulled a pistol from somewhere in his clothes and had it snubbed tidily at Tommy's chest.

"I *said* I will back you up," Sergei repeated.

Tommy felt his face screw up like he was about to cry. The thought was thoroughly humiliating, as bad as peeing his pants. Maybe worse. "Yeah, that's what you told me before. About the kill."

"And I did not lie."

"But—" Tommy's mouth hung open, cheeks sucking in and out like he was some kind of fish. He couldn't think of a single thing to say.

"Merle will see this body. He will laugh and say, 'Oh, that Sergei, he teaches Tommy his crazy way.' And then he will give you another job."

Tommy peered at the Russian. He thought of Crystal's ugly couch squatting in her mom's wet basement. He thought of his KL-65 crushed with a bunch of dirty diapers and milk cartons at the bottom of a landfill.

"And the bonus," Tommy said. "He gives me the bonus. I mean, forty percent. That's what we said last, right? Sixty-forty."

Sergei holstered the pistol, reached up to give Tommy's ear a painful tug. "Oh, this time, one hundred-zero. I did one hundred percent of this hit, yes? And you learn very much from me today. I wish Sergei was my teacher when I was young." Another tug, more painful than the first, and Sergei headed toward the front of the prison with a buoyant stride.

Tommy faltered onto his knees. The stink of smoke filled his nostrils. He brought his rifle around, nosed the tip of the barrel into what remained of the man's left thigh. The skin crackled.

"You dumb fuck."

Tommy squeezed the trigger. The body jerked upward an inch or two, then sank back into its previous position.

"You really thought you were gonna get away? You stupid screw up."

His finger tightened. Relaxed.

He flung the rifle onto the dirt and pulled out his comm, opened a holo connection. No bonus. It was crap, but okay. There'd be a bonus next time. Most important, there *would* be a next time.

"Uncle Merle? Yeah, hey, I've got something to show you." Tommy spoke through numb lips as he blindly glided the holo feed down the length of the smoking corpse. His eyes were wet, his throat thick with mucus. "Check it out," he said. "My first kill."

SOUL SAVER OF SOLEDAD

MORNINGS WERE THE HARDEST.
Prewitt was awake, but kept his eyes closed. He lay in his single bed with a stained comforter pulled to his chin. He got the whiff of something foul, grimaced. In the adjacent apartment, through the thin walls, a child gibbered something about his shoes, and a father responded in low tones, equally unintelligible.

Prewitt brought his left arm up, pressed it across his eyes. The sharp calls of killdeer and scrub-jays mixed with the voices. Spring had just started. Summer birds were a few months away.

He rolled away from the sunlight slipping past the heavy slats of the window blinds. He blew out a gust of breath, groaned a bit, sucked in some more air. After a beat, he forced his matted eyes open and stared at his closet door where a coarse blue uniform jacket and trousers hung, hooked to the top edge. Behind them were the faded sky-blue dress shirt, and a wrinkled necktie that he sometimes wore, though personnel weren't required to at Feldspar.

He needed to get moving or he'd be late for his shift. He didn't want to be late. It wasn't that he cared so much about HR stipulations or a docked paycheck or his watchful coworkers and omniscient supervisor. What he cared about was Alessandra, alone in that cell, counting down the hours and numb with fear. She needed his presence, his compassion, his—

Love. The word uncovered itself. Undeniable, even if he wanted to deny it.

Did he?

No.

When he took the job at Feldspar, he was close to dead inside. One day bled into the next. He moved into the cheapest apartment he could find that was a short driving distance away. He could have biked in if he could fit his wide behind on the saddle. And if he had a bike. The job seemed just like the half-dozen before it, but now he knew better. This was his vocation. God had led him to Feldspar so that he'd be there when Alessandra arrived.

Prewitt shifted on the bed, preparing to sit up. Tingles shot through his arm, and he wriggled his fingers. Something was wrong with his body these days, but he didn't know what. Everything seemed to be quitting on him. On a drive home last week, he'd locked into a coughing fit, and felt pain in his left side, from his armpit in, as if the arteries and veins had gone rock solid. He'd wheeled the pickup to the side of the road and sat there gasping until the urge to hack up a lung passed.

He massaged his scalp. The top of his head had a weird feeling to it as well. Numbness. He brought his chin down to his chest and felt himself choking for breath again. This was the morning routine. Do a survey of all of the body parts. Those you can feel and those you can't. Imagine your heart weaker, the pump having trouble getting blood to all the peripheries. Inside of his mouth, he tongued at a swelling near his pale gums.

He sat up, placed his feet on the carpet and worked his toes into it. Sometimes in the bathtub, he noticed how pale the bottom of his soles had become, and his toes. Maybe it was diabetes. None of his past checkups had indicated a blood sugar problem, but it was a sneaky disease. Or so he'd heard.

When he walked the prison hallways, he had to force himself to tilt his head up, raise his jaw so that the folds of skin wouldn't crush down on that blue collar. Feel the breath not come, and the resulting panic. His lungs forgetting—could they?—to re-inflate. He'd come to the end of an exhale, stuck, waiting on a normal bodily function that was anything but ordinary these days, and start to struggle, to fight for wind. Finally, the relief as it came back to him.

Not even forty years old. A weak vessel, but God had found a use for him, nevertheless.

He picked up his comm, checked the time. It wasn't just Allie. Some of the other inmates needed him too. Needed guidance. Discipline. And a bit more.

He scooped up the crucifix from the nightstand, next to the dog-eared King James, and pressed it to his lips.

He'd always had this designated purpose, for this time, for this country even though he'd lost faith in his vocation during the hard years since Soledad. Oh, he'd still gone through the motions, helping those sad, lost souls to heaven, but mechanically. With hatred for their stubborn ignorance and disgust for their animal crudeness. Not with love.

But Allie was different. She changed things. She changed *him*.

Prewitt Atherton closed his eyes. A prayer became clearer in his mind. He mouthed the words, placing trusted and fervent intent on them for the first time in many years.

∞

The protocol for Alessandra Guillen had been mismanaged from day one.

Deliberately? Just to mess with her head? Prewitt wondered.

Executables were supposed to enter E block during the early morning hours three days prior to release. In Alessandra's case, there had been a delay. Prewitt had the evening shift that day and when he'd arrived, the team had just finished giving her a standard body-cavity search. He stood in the guard room and watched her on camera as she stepped into her holding cell for the first time. She stood listlessly, shoulders drooped, while one officer read her the standard spiel all the Executables got and another did a final sweep of the room for contraband.

After that, she was alone. She sat still on her bunk, hands placed on either side, gripping the thin mattress, staring straight across at the wall. She never looked at the camera.

Prewitt, watching, was half-convinced they'd brought someone's daughter onto the block by mistake. A kid in drab olive coveralls, the standard-issue for inmates at Feldspar. Too large for her by at least a size.

She stood five-feet nothing, maybe weighed 95 pounds out of the shower. Her thick dark hair hung unwashed and limp on her shoulders. He'd leave the monitors, come back, and she'd still be there in view, hands on the blanket or folded against her bent knees. Praying? He couldn't see her lips moving. In another divergence from protocol, Feldspar hadn't bothered to offer her a meeting with the clergy of her choice.

Maybe, when she sat there like that, she was simply waiting?

Two more days.

Two more days for her heart to beat, her lungs to work. Two days before it was all over. Thinking about it brought that mysterious pain to his side again. Something like an enormous cramp immobilized his chest and he struggled to breathe.

Her crime had been notorious in the state, her trial a temporary media sensation driven by her petite and fragile beauty, the social status, money and good looks of the man she'd killed, and—of course—the sheer bloodiness of the murder. The victim's family had made clear to the press that they'd already ponied up to hire an execution company to kill Allie as soon as she left penitentiary grounds.

Six Executables waited in Cell Block E for imminent release and she was the only damn one of them who was going to die. The rest were skinwastes and addicts who'd come up from the gutter just long enough to help out America's corporations by slaving in a prison factory for a few years. Upon release, they'd sink right back into that same gutter. Even though their punishment supposedly would continue since they'd leave prison stripped of citizenship and basic rights and the ability to hold a legitimate job, none of that mattered much. They'd go right back to their drugs, whoring, and robbery, their child-creation, child-torment and child-desertion. They'd walk out of Feldspar and a car would pull up to the front, friends or family or pimps come to ferry them back to the underbellies of Winnemucca, Tahoe, Vegas. Life would go on in that petri dish. Nobody cared enough to make them pay the ultimate price for their crimes.

They didn't need help from the likes of Prewitt Atherton.

Allie did, even if—so far—she refused to admit it.

"Disgusting," spat one of the female guards—Kreizmueller, Prewitt thought that was her name—staring at the monitor and commenting to no one in particular.

"We looking at the same thing?" a male guard named Givings asked. "Or you talking about what she did?"

Kreizmueller turned in her chair and glared at them. "I'm talking about men. The way you watch her. I'm asking what it is that you'd find attractive about someone who looks like she's about twelve years old. What a man who's six-foot-whatever could find desirable about a person who maybe comes up to here on him." She held her hand as high as her thick bosom.

"She don't look that young," said Givings.

"The hell she doesn't."

"Nah. You're just jealous because you're more on the big-boned side."

"Nice, Givings," Kreizmueller said. "Creep like you goes for that type, likes them dressing in little Catholic schoolgirl skirts without any underwear on, shaving it raw—"

"That's the way you scissor sisters like them, maybe." Givings stuck two fingers to his mouth and made a crude gesture with his tongue.

Prewitt paid them no mind. Let the dead bury the dead and the vulgar sink into their vulgarity. He fixated on the solitary figure on the bunk. He recognized the slow sinking of the chin to the chest, the folding down of the shoulders as if the whole world was caving in on her. A common position: getting used to the idea that she only had a few hours left in this world, and dreading a greater unknown: exactly how she was going to meet her Maker. It was most assuredly going to be violent. You hoped for quick. But execution companies didn't have to be quick. Sometimes they were specifically contracted to take their sweet goddamned time. If Allie despaired, he didn't blame her.

He knew about despair.

∞

Feldspar was another edition in a cookie-cutter assembly line of for-profit prisons in a booming industry that had taken over any number of depressed small towns of America. From them, Prewitt had found steady work, and nobody asked too many questions from his former employers about his habits, moods, eccentricities, or any unusual circumstances that had preceded his departures.

One or two of the early ones had been more than waystations for him. He'd stayed a couple of years in Montana, three in northern California. But after Soledad, he'd lost his taste for the work. Lost heart. Since then, the vast majority had been no more than a year and meant nothing more to him than a paycheck. He drifted on the wind, to the next post, the next job. Four months at Feldspar—he already felt like he'd overstayed his time. Except for Allie.

He had to do right by her. God demanded it.

As he drove his small Ford sedan down the two-lane road that led to the prison, his hand trembled on the steering wheel. Was his hand shaking at the thought of seeing her again, or was this just another in a myriad of symptoms? Or did that even matter anymore?

The scrub and steppe of the Great Basin Desert stretched away on either side. About a half-mile to the east, a ridge rose up from the flat scrub.

Sometimes, when the day neared for the release of one of the more high-profile Executables, he'd look that direction and see the scum of the earth gathered on that ridge, settling in to wait. They'd mill about their piece-of-shit pickup trucks and jeeps, their four-wheelers, cans of beer in their hands. One or two of them with binoculars, spying on the oversized gates. Waiting, always waiting. The worst of the human race, right there, like hungry wolves pacing, ready for the approach of human caribou.

They were even worse, by his reckoning, than the professionals from the execution companies who kept it low-key and on-task when they assembled a few hours before a scheduled release. The professionals were doing a legal job for pay. The low-lifes were there to party, enjoy the spectacle of torture, and try to horn in on the action themselves. Carving Crews, they called themselves. If he could have called down a curse on every last one of their heads, he would have done it.

His Ford followed the road, curving away from the ridge. And then: there it was.

Feldspar, a seventy-acre island of pale walls constructed of massive concrete blocks, was striking in appearance for its twelve gun-towers lording above the ground like alien silos, and its twelve-foot perimeter fences topped by rolls of razor wire. Forbidding was the best word to describe the facility from the outside.

On the inside? Methodical. Efficient and budget-savvy. The corporations had bought and paid for the right to oversee the penal chores of the country, and put those idle hands to work for a few cents by the hour. Feldspar was only a higher tech version of Angola or Parchman Farm. Instead of picking cotton, the inmates put their hands in God-knew what, in tasks that shifted each time the company did a re-fit on the line.

Prewitt stopped his car at the gate, pausing for the authorization to enter from another guard in the tower looming overhead. He sighed. Sometimes—mornings, usually—it took a while for someone to answer the call. It seemed like it was taking longer every shift. He wondered if he had an enemy stationed in every tower and at every hallway nexus. His coworkers tolerated him, but he knew they didn't really like him.

While he waited, he looked out across the desert and thought about Allie's chances.

∞

All the corrections officers walked the same hallways, but he was the only one who got saddled with the nicknames. The usual ones, sure, like Lard Ass and Land Whale. Others got under his skin a bit more: Ghoul, Angel of Death, Crypt Keeper. Then there was the one that stuck: Soul Saver. The Soul Saver of Soledad. Someone had got into his work file, found his resume there and worked backwards online, found out about his stint in Soledad, California.

They were uttered in hushed whispers as he passed, of course. Few of the guards spoke to him at all. Captain Grey, his boss, mainly. Only Givings ever conversed with him on a regular basis. He was a rat-faced little punk, with moles on his neck and a nose that looked to have been broken more than a few times.

"You know, I've read about guys like you," Givings said in the cafeteria once, plunking down his tray, leaning in without being asked. "Nurses, working in old folks' homes or the VA. Yeah, one of them slipped the needle to like over 300 geezers, they think. Overdosed them."

Prewitt kept his eyes on his food, the fork sliding through slithery noodles.

"Word travels, bud. You can't outrun who you are, Prewitt. And they are going to nail you to the cross one of these days for what you're doing."

∞

"Guillen," Prewitt tried again, this time with more authority. But Alessandra lay on her bunk faced away from the door. Prewitt only had authority to enter her cell if he suspected she harbored a weapon or was attempting to take her life. He considered going in there anyway, but the thought of Givings and the other guards gawking on the monitors stopped him.

He rapped on the door with his baton again, biting his lip as he watched through a narrow slot at eye level. A tray of food, untouched, was on the small ledge where he'd left it a half-hour earlier. He'd seen this before. Sometimes inmates deliberately weakened themselves before release. Sometimes they were just so damn scared that their stomachs stopped working properly

He tried again, his face pressed to the door, his eyes at the access slot. "Alessandra." No response. He cut a glance sideways at the nearest camera and squared his shoulders, raised his chin, trying to make himself look tougher. Just a hard-nosed guard giving an Executable a little more shit in her life.

"Allie." His voice softer. Tender, even.

She rolled over finally so that she faced the door, and him. Her gaze met his and his tongue went dry in his mouth. She looked smaller and thinner than ever, curled on the mattress. Her face had a hollowed-out look and circles cut shadows under her eyes, but somehow that only gave her a delicate beauty that twisted his heart. Sometimes, when he saw a moth or a firefly on a warm summer night, he felt something similar. Because something so lovely was here and then—sshhtt—gone.

Alessandra's gaze slid away. Like he was just another person in the world who had given up on her. More than anything, Prewitt wanted to unbolt the door, kneel by the bunk, and look straight into her dark eyes. Touch her hands, cup the side of her face.

But he was as close as he could get. He threw another reflexive glance at the camera before he could stop himself. "You should eat," he said. He couldn't say anything he really wanted to say, anything that really mattered.

Alessandra offered the barest shrug. Her collarbones pressed against her skin.

"Of all the ways to kill yourself, you're picking the hardest," Prewitt said, looking away, rubbing the top of his left hand with his right. There was a small growth near his middle finger. It'd changed color, gone much paler since the last time he'd bothered with it. "And, anyway, it's too slow. You don't have time."

"I'm not," she said, barely above a whisper.

"What's that?"

"I said I'm not," she repeated, slightly louder, and pushed herself into a sitting position. "I'm not killing myself."

"Sure you are. I've seen it before. If you don't eat, then when they release you—" He didn't want to be cruel, but she needed to understand. "No stamina to run. All over."

"I'm not killing myself," she repeated, looking down. He admired the natural length of her dark lashes. The edges of her eyes were red from stress, but no sty or cyst threatened to burst from infection. He seemed to get those on a monthly basis. He was struck again at how small she was. It just didn't match up to the crime. Her arms, collarbone, neck—so thin, he could snap those bones.

"Eat," he commanded, feeling foolish. Who was he to issue commands? Who listened to him? "There's some protein in it," he explained. "Not a lot, but you'll need every bit of it. That is—if you're going to go through with it."

She laughed. Bitterness ate like rust at its edges. It made Prewitt sad. He wondered what her laugh sounded like when she was happy. He wished he could hear that. "It's not like I have a choice," she said.

"Maybe you do. I can help you." He realized he was checking the camera again. Damnit! He had to stop doing that. It made him look guilty of something. No way Givings wouldn't notice. "I've done it before."

She stared at him, honestly perplexed, which only tightened the ache in his chest. That sort of innocence . . . it wasn't something you encountered in a place like this. "Done what?" she asked.

He shifted his weight from one foot to the other, and kept his voice low enough that she had to come closer. She stepped slowly toward the door, pausing halfway between it and the cot. An unfamiliar yearning moved through him like blood through his veins. It was as if his very flesh was praying—or maybe begging—for her to come right up to the door. Near enough that he could touch her face, run a hand along her hair.

"I've helped girls out," he murmured. She strained her neck forward, the muscles taut, as she listened. "Girls that were trapped. Like you are. I can get you something. Something painless. It'll just look like you had a heart attack. They'll think it was from the stress. It happens."

She was quiet for a beat. He watched her, his gaze fluttering up and down her face, looking for—

gratitude? Acknowledgement? But when she spoke, it was without emotion. "A capsule."

"Right. Comes in a couple of pills, down it with a glass of water. And then it's done." He was speaking too rapidly. Like he was afraid the words would refuse to come out of his mouth unless he pushed them out fast. The pain in his chest twisted another notch when he thought of her collapsed on the floor of this dismal little room, a half-empty cup of water beside the bed.

He didn't want to think of her like that. But to think of her outside, running toward that ridge, toward the killers and the Carving Crews was even worse. The ruin they'd make of her—

Allie took a deep breath. He thought she was considering his offer, but then she surprised him by declining outright. "No. That's telling the world I'm guilty," she said. "I didn't murder anyone. I didn't kill my little girl's father. Murdering myself would put all of that in doubt. I'm not going to have my daughter grow up with more stigma."

She didn't understand. He had to be blunt. "Alessandra . . . Allie . . . the world already thinks you're guilty. What happens when you're released, well, the world thinks you'll be getting what you deserve. The family—" He let out a slow breath, hating to bring her this bit of news. "They've hired an execution company. Regency. One of the higher quality outfits."

She gave him a quizzical look.

"Higher quality," he clarified, "meaning they rarely miss. I don't want to be cruel, but . . . you aren't going to have a fair chance when you walk out of here. This is no fifty-fifty odds kind of situation."

The muscles in her face suddenly twitched and quirked like she'd lost all control of them. Desolation filled her eyes. Prewitt could barely swallow. Surely she already knew all this. It couldn't be a surprise. But hearing it said out loud, by another human being, made it real. Why did he have to be the one to do that to her?

"I'm sorry," he whispered, wretched. This was his vocation? It felt like nothing but a burden, a misery of tonnage strapped to his back and about to break him. He wanted to hold her, but instead he drove another nail into her thoughts.

"And your daughter . . . everybody's already forgotten about her."

"I haven't." The look she flung at him then was pure anger. He shriveled under it. Knew that he deserved it. But an instant later, her face crumpled. She struggled to speak and the words stumbled out in a jerky, halting succession. "It's just, I can't—stand the thought—her being—an orphan."

Prewitt's face quivered. His hand went to the lock at the edge of the cell door. He was on the brink, at the edge of the cliff. And they were watching him, somebody always watching. He'd stood here too long already, but he couldn't make himself walk away. He lowered his hand to his side and closed his eyes until he thought he had himself under control again.

"Where does she live?" he asked.

Allie raised her shoulders. Her face contorted and she took a shuddering breath. "I don't know."

Outrage flooded Prewitt's bloodstream like an intravenous drug. "They wouldn't tell you?" But he knew the answer already. Of course they wouldn't bother telling her something like that. She was an Executable, not a human being.

"I have a sister in Sacramento," Allie said. "At least, I did. But I don't know if they sent Deirdra there or not. They maybe just stuck her in a foster home, I don't know." Her left hand worked at her throat. "It's just really hard to think of her in that kind of—" She broke off.

"I was a foster kid." Prewitt spoke without thinking and immediately wondered: Should he have told her? This had never been a part of his vocation. He listened to the Executables, advised them, prayed with them, brought them the little white capsules if they wanted that. He never talked about himself.

Allie stared at him. "Was it . . . okay?"

"I ran away from them."

"Oh, God."

"It wasn't that bad." He spoke quickly, afflicted with the need to comfort her.

"Bad enough you ran away!"

"I was a teenager. Seventeen when I left. And they weren't terrible. They didn't hurt me. They were just . . . kind of cold. I didn't want to be there anymore. So I left."

"Jesus."

He never should have told her. "But there are good places too. And—how old is she? Deirdra?"

"She'd be eight now."

"I'll find out for you." What was wrong with him? His mouth kept saying things without consulting his brain. "I'll find out where she is. I'll tell you before . . ."

Allie swung three quick steps toward him. She was so close to the door now that if he'd put his hand through the slot, he could have touched her. He didn't move.

"If she's in foster care," Allie said, leaning in even closer, oh my God, so close, "can you make sure she gets to my sister? Jenny MacKenzie in Sacramento."

Prewitt was nodding. "Yes," he heard himself say. "I promise."

What was he doing? But Allie smiled now, the first time he'd seen her smile. It lit up her face. He'd never seen anyone more beautiful.

He heard activity down at the far end of the corridor. Metal sliding over metal; footsteps on hard tile. He'd stood here far too long already, but . . . she was still smiling. At *him*.

Your vocation, he reminded himself and clenched his eyes shut briefly to sever himself from that bright face. Instead, against the darkness of his eyelids, he watched a woman slowly butchered by a pair of killers from Eye for an Eye Agency while the Carving Crews encircling the scene yipped and hoisted their beers.

He opened his eyes. Time to focus.

"Alessandra. You—look. The capsules. You'll want to do this. You won't feel anything at all. You just go to sleep. And you wake up in a better world than this. I mean, you believe in God and heaven. I saw in your file, you requested a priest. You're one of His flock. He's calling you home. Do it this way. Don't put it in their hands."

She was already shaking her head.

His voice intensified. "What they'll do to you, you can't imagine. They do the most horrible things to the women." He couldn't bear the thought of her dead body. He couldn't bear the thought of killers swarming around her.

"I'll bring them tomorrow," he said and glanced down the corridor. One of the new guards was at the first cell, taking a gander through the slot.

"No, I—"

"You can lie down on the bed. Peaceful. Quiet. Take the pills. No one will be any wiser. I can do this. It's— it's like I was called into your life, just at this time, for this purpose. Please, Alessandra."

"No. It's a sin."

Sin? He could choke on the word. Sin was this world and the human animals that ran through it.

"It's not," he protested. "Not in these circumstances."

"What you're talking about, it's just the body," she said and Prewitt could have wept at her naiveté. "What I care about now is my soul. My soul and my little girl."

"You don't know—"

"Yes. I do." Her voice was firm. "I know this is no-win. But I'll die my way, with dignity."

Prewitt closed his eyes, shook his head. "You have no idea what can happen to you out there. That's the last place to look for dignity."

"I guess," she said. "I guess I'll settle for integrity, then."

∞

Kreizmueller eyed him strangely when he entered the monitor room at the nexus. "Don't hang around that cell like that again unless you want me to report it to Captain Grey," she said.

Prewitt looked at Allie on the monitor. She'd returned to her bunk and lay on it, rolled away from the camera again. "I was trying to get her to eat."

"Sure, sure. That's what you were doing." Kreizmueller smirked. "And saving a soul, while you were at it?" She rummaged in some plastic packaging on the desk and pulled out a yellow marshmallow peep. That's right, Easter was only two weeks away. He'd forgotten. He usually just worked the holidays, got the overtime.

He ignored her, puzzling at his conversation with Allie. "She claims she never killed anybody."

"They all say that."

"She—doesn't look big enough to do anything to anybody."

"Obviously a jury came to a different conclusion."

"But you watched it. When it was on the streams, you watched the whole trial, right?"

"Enough of it."

"So the evidence was completely conclusive, that she shot—"

"Stabbed. Baby Daddy was stabbed. A lot."

"But he was a big guy, wasn't he? She's so small. To bring him down like that—"

"Only had to get the first couple of slices in by surprise. After that, he was probably flat on his stomach bleeding out or on his back blocking the knife with his hands or curled up and praying to Christ. Your options aren't real great, no matter how short your attacker is. And once you're down—" She made a hacking motion with her right arm.

53

∞

He'd tried to talk to Givings about what Alessandra had said, to feel him out about things, while they stood outside at their cars in the parking lot. But the conversation ended up haunting his drive home and while he tried to choke down another frozen dinner.

"So how'd you get all high-and-mighty, Mr. Soul Saver?" Givings cracked, shaking his head. "Who are you, suddenly questioning the juries? Courts found her guilty as hell. She got the sentence she deserved, she did the time she was required to, and now she's getting released and she'll get what's coming to her. That's how it works. She doesn't like it, she should've thought of that before she did that slice-and-dice on the dentist."

"But the kid—"

"Yeah, yeah, the kid. Daughter, right? She claimed the guy was the father. Funny thing, though, when they did the DNA test? Turned out he wasn't. And he was tired of her trying to railroad him into paying support for her, so he was cutting her off. That's the story, Prewitt. That's why it all went down."

"I just don't see how—"

"She wanted him to keep paying for the kid, he was putting a stop to it, so she went Manson Family on his ass. He had so many stab wounds, there was chunks of him all over the goddamn bathroom. I'm not kidding, Prewitt, even in the can. It's all over the net. Pull up the autopsy vids. But unless you did time working in a butcher shop, you're not going to like looking at 'em." He grinned.

Jesus. And they called Prewitt 'The Ghoul'.

"Bottom line," Givings said, swinging open his car door and reaching inside to pluck a fast food bag off the driver's seat. "What comes up like a giant red flag is a crime of passion, Prewitt. If it was like she said, her alibi? Hitman comes in, boom, entry wound under the armpit on the left side, straight into the ticker. Or right in the back, into the kidneys, you get me? Quick and clean. Nothing like this. Somebody was taking out a lot of frustration on this guy. And for what? He pulled a wrong tooth?"

Givings shrugged and tossed the bag on the back seat. "Look at you, being sucked in by her. Same as the dentist. Difference is, you got the walls between you and her, protecting your dumb ass from the chop-chop."

That night, Prewitt churned among his sheets, kicking out, knocking his pillows to the floor. He shouldn't believe her. He'd never believed a killer before. Yet he felt something was wrong. The evidence—planted? Faked? Was he really just a sucker, like Givings suggested? Was she manipulating him? Was that really so hard for him to accept?

Yes. It was.

But that didn't mean it wasn't true.

He could talk to her about it, but did it matter?

Tomorrow was her final day. He was working evening shift when she'd be down to her last hours. The wolves would be gathering on the ridge. He'd be able to see them when he drove in.

He pulled open the drawer of his nightstand and got out the pills. His stomach turned over, as queasy as if he'd just downed poison himself.

∞

Prewitt stopped at her cell door, slid the narrow slot open, and called out to her. He was surprised to find her away from her bunk, like she'd been waiting for him.

"Did you find out about Deirdra?" she asked.

He paused, guilt worming through him. He'd been so focused on trying to sort out whether she was guilty or innocent and how to get her to take the pills and save herself that he'd broken his promise.

"I'm working on it," he lied. But it wasn't really a lie because he would work on it as soon as he finished checking on the inmates and went back to the monitoring station.

It was terrible, watching the light in her eyes fade out.

"Oh," was all she said. One simple word like a knife to his gut.

"You know, it might help me find her if I had a few more details. Names. Her father's name was—?"

Allie gave him a sidelong look. It killed him, seeing that edge of mistrust.

"I promise you," Prewitt said, his voice full and trembling, a river pushing up toward the edges of its banks. "I promise you, I'll find out and I will tell you."

She stared at him a good long moment, then finally nodded. But her shoulders were low again, caving in. He wondered if she really wanted to talk to him or if she simply felt she had no other options. Which she didn't.

"Reece was a good man," she was telling him a minute later. "Good to me. Good to Deirdra. We'd had our problems, but we'd worked through them. And even at the end, when I knew we couldn't stay together any more, there wasn't any bitterness."

She watched Prewitt intently. "Do you believe me? You're a good man, too, I can tell. You haven't quit on the world like so many have. There aren't so many people left who haven't been sickened by everything. But you're different, somehow. You still believe in something. Is it God? Is it Jesus? Do you still pray to Him, Prewitt?"

"Yes." He studied the shapes her mouth made as it formed her words.

"Okay. Well. The last night Reece and I talked on the comm, he said he had a meeting in a few hours with a man who wanted him to relocate his business to Carson City. He didn't want to do it, but the money. The money was supposed to be so good, he couldn't say no. And it meant we would be apart, and that made him crazy with worry, because he loved Deirdra so much. And I think, Prewitt, I think, you know, he still loved me, too. And I loved him so much."

Prewitt just nodded, over and over, an understanding smile tight against his face and a burning at the back of his eyes. What would it be like, to hear her say those words, but about him? What would that feel like?

"I know that sounds insane, you don't believe it, but—just a part of me, of us, thought we could still work things out, somehow. For Deirdra. To keep us all together."

"I don't know. I didn't know him," Prewitt stammered.

"The other thing. Reece was involved in something he didn't want me to press him on, but it had to do with a politician in the city. It wasn't that he owed him money. There—there'd been some kind of a relationship, when they were in college together. And Reece told me something about being threatened, and he pushed back, and they thought he might be trying to blackmail them. And I think, that's probably what happened to him, that they tricked him with this meeting. That they killed him and made it look like it was me. And they're the ones that have arranged . . . what you see outside. I'm a loose end, Prewitt. They get rid of me, forever."

"Did you say any of this at your trial? Did you tell anybody?"

"I've tried, Prewitt. I've tried, for years, but once it was on the net, there was only one story, one version that anyone would ever accept. And I made a mess of things on the witness stand. My lawyer was horrible. I got so confused, I started mixing things up and he never stopped me and it was all being recorded. I wasn't right in my head, Prewitt, do you understand? Do you understand how something like that could happen to someone like me?" Her gaze was fervent, locking onto his own, almost willing him to believe her story. And damned if it wasn't working.

∞

He looked at the little girl in the photograph. She'd been about four-years-old when it'd been taken. It was easy to see Allie's genetic contributions: the shape of her brown eyes, her small aquiline nose, her dark-brown hair, long and straight. But he didn't see much of Reece Daniels there. The ears, maybe? A divot birthmark, a notch in the lobe? Perhaps the chin. But no. Just looking at the picture, Prewitt could see little of the dentist's rugged good looks in Deirdra's face.

And Daniels had been a handsome man. Tall. Fit-looking with muscular shoulders. Great teeth, of course, but what else would you expect from a dentist? And don't forget, a serious career, an actual profession, nothing like being an hourly-wage guard jumping from penitentiary to penitentiary every year.

Prewitt brought the pictures of Deirdra and Daniels close to his face to scrutinize them. No, not much resemblance. So if you can't see it, that means he probably couldn't see it, either, Prewitt thought. It's like Givings said. He went with the paternity angle until it was obvious she wasn't his kid, and the charade had to end. It had to end.

∞

"I won't do it," she said, turning the pair of capsules over in her hands, the pills Prewitt had just pushed through the slot in the door. "I already told you," she whispered.

She was so close to him now that he could feel the warmth of her breath, could smell her hair.

And all he could think of was Soledad, a couple hundred meters outside the prison grounds. The woman's flayed skin. The smashed bones. A mess of blood between her legs. He'd prayed with that woman in her cell while she'd laughed at him and cussed and told him that if he really wanted to help her, he could sneak in some poison or a razor blade. And he'd refused. But after he'd been called out to help remove her body when the cut-rate execution company hadn't bothered to haul it away—the first time he'd ever seen an Executable after the killing—his soul went numb. His fire went out. He researched pharmaceuticals and poisons and ferried them to the Executables, starting with several at Soledad before he was asked to move on.

And it brought him no joy. Just an emptiness that started near his straining lungs and his paralyzed heart and gradually expanded, oozing out between his ribs and eroding everything it touched.

"Please," he said to Alessandra, no longer knowing what he was asking from her.

"No." She shook her head. "It would be like admitting that I'd murdered Deirdra's father. I'm innocent of that. And I won't be guilty of this crime, either. And you. Prewitt. You talk about having this calling, this vocation. You need to stop pushing death on people. You need to start giving life."

He knew they were watching on the monitors, but he didn't care. He slid the larger panel up, the one where they pushed the dinner trays through, and put his hand inside with a shuddering breath. His rational mind— what remained of it—told him to stop. Anything could happen. She'd been convicted of a brutal murder, for God's sake, and it was possible that she'd even done it.

But when he felt her soft warm hand in his, their fingers clasped, entwined. Just touching. Human contact. He hadn't known such a thing in so long, he barely had a memory of it. His mother, before she died two days after his seventh birthday. She'd always hugged him, snuggled him deep in her lap, curled on his bed with him until he fell asleep. His father—dead of a sudden heart-attack when Prewitt was twelve—was the opposite. Gray-haired, with matching pale eyes, and a dull monotone. His father had never been young. He was always hunched. Gravity pulling him into a grave.

Prewitt knelt, right there in the corridor. He had both of her hands in his now. He felt the welts, the scars from the brutal work the convicts had been doing in the factory, tracing some as far up as her elbows. He brought her palms to his face, against his cheeks. He brushed them with his lips, tasted her flesh, the salt, could smell her scent through the cheap soap.

He heard her breathing quicken, felt her hands in his hair, brushing the overgrown strands behind his ears. He took her hands again, kissing them full on. He was oblivious to cameras, to prying eyes, to the sights and sounds of other Executables in their rows of holding cells stretching the length of the hallway.

∞

He was surprised to see Captain Grey in the control room. He never worked this late on a weeknight. Prewitt's face flushed as he thought about what had happened at Alessandra's cell. At how much the Captain may have witnessed.

"You off tomorrow, Atherton?" Grey asked, not looking at him, staring with those gunmetal-blue eyes of his at various rows of cameras recording inmate movement. "You've sure done a lot of overtime this month."

"Yes, sir."

The Captain nodded once, firmly, without looking at him. "Guess we'll see you in a couple of days, then," he finally added.

∞

No one had to die today.

Prewitt didn't want to have to kill anyone.

He wasn't even planning to use the gun if he didn't have to.

He parked his car in the cul-de-sac of a residential neighborhood. The prison was a good piece of walking, but he felt as though he had purpose, and it would take him as far as he needed to go.

He stuck to the main roads as long as he dared, but as the east began to glow with the coming dawn, he headed into the scrub. He wore old hiking boots, dark sweatpants and shirt, and the holster, carrying the 9mm handgun that normally was shelved in a nightstand in his bedroom. The desert air was still chill; he could make out the morning campfires of the Carving Crews, could smell the brew of the coffee in pots on a grill over the open flames. He saw shadows of men emerging from tents, shoving on boots and pushing arms and heads through shirt tops.

He'd trained himself to use the weapon. He'd taken the courses, stood at a range firing on targets at various distances. He was a good target shooter. People had told him that. And the weapon was for self-defense. You couldn't be too careful nowadays.

∞

Prewitt had never been gifted with athleticism. The only thing his parents had handed down to him was a predisposition to asthma, a condition that had plagued him during childhood. When they'd run the mile to try to win a medal for physical fitness in elementary school, there was no question where Prewitt Atherton was going to wind up. He'd finished once, dead last but still moving his legs. That was his Arc de Triomphe moment. He'd raised his arms, looked up directly, past the blazing sun and into a blue cloudless sky, and sent a thank-you to the Almighty right there, under the hectoring and jeers from the small peanut gallery that seemed to haunt him during that time period, the tormentors who were the only ones who ever took an interest. He never knew his time for that run. The coach with the stopwatch had already sauntered off to get everyone in line to head back into the building.

No, he was never going to win a medal. There was the pull-up bar, a nemesis. He couldn't do a single repetition.

In middle school, it was more of the same, and worse. A coach screaming at him—"Come on, Prunella!"—as he tried to haul himself up a rope to the ceiling but not even getting a foot off the ground, feeling his t-shirt ride up, revealing his oversized belly and man nipples to his many admirers. The wrestling unit, where he lost to the smallest runt in the school, mercifully pinned in 12 seconds.

And finally freshman year in high school, where on the first day of the required gym class, he ended up lovingly shoved into a locker, courtesy of the boys whose daddies all knew one another at the country club.

∞

Prewitt struggled up a rock outcropping, dragging himself over the lip, then lay there, trembling and exhausted. He peeked at the executioners' camp, and took a look at the sky. Mid-morning would be the time of Alessandra's release, which gave him at least a couple of hours to put his plan together and to catch his breath. He shivered in his clothes, damp with his sweat, especially in the middle of his back.

He knew he should have figured this out already. You don't wait until the helicopter drops you in country to come up with a strategy. Problem was, he'd tried to get his head around it all night and, no matter what angle he used to come at the situation, he came up with zilch.

Try to take out the professional killers? Ridiculous, and if they didn't get him, the Carving Crews would. Take out the Carving Crews? Hell, the pros would murder Allie and give Prewitt a tip of the hat on their way out, a thank you for getting rid of the scum.

Which left exactly one other angle, as far as he could tell. A single murder or maybe a murder-suicide. Which didn't strike him as much of a plan, certainly not one to be proud of. And not one that Allie would approve.

Able to breathe again, he craned forward to check the Regency camp. He counted at least six men around the fire, but he had three full magazines of bullets; plenty of ammunition if he needed it. He took the handgun from the holster, pulled the slide back to engage a round, and ejected the magazine as he'd been taught, replacing it with a full one. The gun was made of polymer, incredibly light. Still had a popping recoil, though. He had to remember that. He put the safety on and worked his way back down the rock to the ground, hunching over, gasping a little.

He'd take fifteen minutes to rest. Then make his way—

If the sun had been setting, he might have seen them from their shadows, coming up behind him. Instead, the only warning he got was a clearing of the throat, and the sound of shoes on loose rocks. He froze, then slowly turned his head, just enough to make out the tall figure of Captain Grey standing directly behind him. Givings knelt beside the Captain, holding a rifle leveled directly at Prewitt's head. The thought of a fight dissipated when Givings chambered a round into the long gun.

"Atherton. Pleasant morning for a hike," Grey said, smoothing his short hair back. He extended his hand palm flat, then beckoned with his fingers, indicating Prewitt's gun. "You won't be needing that any more today. I'd like it in my possession, if you don't mind."

Again, Prewitt had the urge to put up a fight. And just as quickly, Givings seemed to read his thoughts, snuggling closer to the stock and tapping an index finger nearer the trigger. "Don't try it, Prewitt. I'll blow your pretty head off."

"Let's put the sidearm in the holster, shall we?" Grey asked, firmly but without any malice in his voice. "And then hand it to me, gently. That's it. I'm assuming you have a permit for this weapon?"

Prewitt nodded. Alessandra's release was still hours away. He thought of his car, how long it would take to jog back to it, hopeful that it would still be in time for—

A rescue?

"Stand down, Givings. We need to de-escalate. Cooler heads prevail," the Captain said, tucking the weapon under his arm. "Prewitt, you know it is illegal to have a weapon like this on the prison grounds, right? I have due cause for your dismissal."

"We're not on the grounds, sir," Prewitt offered, weakly.

The Captain gave a little smile, nodded, and indicated Prewitt was to walk in front of him, back along a dirt path toward the asphalt road. Back toward Feldspar.

"You're close enough, though. My word against yours. Our eyewitness, Officer Givings here, will attest to intent."

When they reached the car, the Captain placed Prewitt's gun in the backseat, then straightened up next to the driver's side door. He held up a palm, showing two small pills in his palm.

"I'm not even going to ask you what these are, or how they came to be in the possession of the Executable due to be released shortly," he said, before letting them drop and crushing them under his heel into the black tar road. "But I do want you to answer a few questions, if you'd be so kind. Back in my office. Get in. Up front, if you would. Givings, let's unload both of these weapons."

"Captain, I—" Prewitt started, but the rest of the sentence died on his lips when he saw the front gate of the prison open, and three figures emerge on the outer walk. The shortest of the three took the lead, walking across the pick-up lane and out into the xeriscape that marked the border of Feldspar.

No car sat idling, waiting to pick her up. No surprise there.

Alessandra was on her own.

"Givings, help Atherton into the car."

"What's going on?" Prewitt sagged, his left hand reaching out, clutching the roof of Grey's official car. "It's too soon. You can't release her this early!"

"She's a special case, Prewitt. Different rules apply."

One of the men trailing Alessandra was a wretched-looking priest, reading from a book, lifting his arm and making the sign of the cross. For a brief moment, Allie stumbled. Then she bolted, heading full bore toward a rise to the east of the prison. She pumped her arms and legs hard, running as fast as she could.

Prewitt fought past Givings, stumbling down the road's embankment. "Run!" he screamed at the top of his lungs at the fleeing figure. "Run! Allie! Goddamnit!" Givings dove at his legs and Prewitt fell hard, rolling several feet to the ground below. The Captain knelt beside the two men, placing a hand on Prewitt's shoulder, pressing him to the earth.

"No! No! Captain, please . . . please stop it, please . . ."

She'd almost crested the ridge when they got to her. The wolves closed quickly. In seconds, she was down, and they converged. He couldn't make out much more as sand was kicked up and dust covered whatever atrocity they'd planned. His insides quaked when he heard her faint screams. He dropped his head to the ground, squeezed his eyelids closed.

They do the most horrible things to the women—

∞

"Fraternization is a natural hazard in a profession like ours, Atherton," the Captain said as he drove them away. "It's understandable, it happens, and if that was all it was, I could even forgive you for it. I wouldn't necessarily report it as is, and it's something I could sugarcoat in the paperwork, maybe get you a week off without pay as suspension, and that would be the end of it. But this other thing you were doing—no, this I cannot accept. You stepped over a line, son. It's an attempt to thwart justice."

Prewitt slumped in the car seat, head hung to his chest. "Nothing out there can in any way be called justice," he said in a deadened voice.

"Shh, Prewitt, shh. She ain't screeching no more. It's over," Givings said.

"You don't know that. You can't say that, she's probably gagged and they're carting her away somewhere, goddamnit—Captain, please, for God's sake—"

"It's gone plenty quiet."

"Givings," the Captain said, shooting him a look in the rearview mirror.

"We just watched. We just sat there and watched it," Prewitt continued. He pressed his face into his dirty hands, smeared them across his eyes.

"You take your act down the road to Lovelock, Prewitt," Givings said. "Give those pills of yours to the kiddie rapers and tell'em it's saltpeter. You'd be doing us all a favor."

"Three days, Givings—and I don't mean a long weekend—you open your yap again," the Captain warned, looking into the back seat.

"Yes, sir."

The Captain braked the car, shifted into neutral, and turned toward Prewitt.

"If the warden knew what I was about to do, he'd hand me my ass. He'd say I was kicking the can down the road, passing the problem on to somebody else. Which I'm guessing is how we ended up with you here. Someone getting shed of you, you moving on. But I don't see any reason to make this anything more than what it appears to me. Illegal firearm on the prison grounds. Fair enough. And not an offense to keep a man from earning his living."

They drove to the gate and gained entrance almost instantly.

∞

The tiny black shopping cart at the Dollar Discount barely fit through the aisle at the front of the dingy low-lit store, and Prewitt felt his body brush against merchandise as he twisted his way through. Few customers took note of him as he stopped in front of the gifts marked down for the upcoming Easter holiday. A mannequin of a young girl—with wide eyes, dark skin, dark hair, and a mouth set in a permanent smile—sat atop a cornucopia of chocolate eggs, jelly beans, and plastic grass. She was dressed all in pink, shirt and shorts.

Prewitt closed his eyes, hesitated. He brought a hand up, squeezed gently between his eyes. He was in his civvies, out of a job again, in a small desert town whose largest employer had just deemed him no longer necessary to operations. They gave him a month severance. Damn generous of them, all things considered.

But there were others who would hire him.

He had some idea of where to find Alessandra's daughter. Her file—well. There'd been an address, but it wasn't Sacramento. It was in Des Moines. Which meant he was Iowa-bound.

Those files—

Forensic reports, histories. Facts, sure. But a lot of fairy tales in them, too.

He picked up the cellophane-wrapped basket and put it into the cart. There was no way he would ever be Deirdra's legal guardian, he understood that, but he intended to make sure she got to her aunt's in California and had a chance at a decent life.

Think of it as a new vocation, one that would make Allie happy.

He massaged the flesh of his forehead where a headache brewed. He couldn't bear to think about Allie. Not yet.

He paid the lady at the cash register with his cash card. Apparently Feldspar had come through with a necessary deposit.

She smiled at him. "For your daughter?" she asked, quite friendly. Surprisingly so. He grunted at her "Have a nice day" and carried his purchase toward the door.

Daughter. No.

Not exactly.

But Prewitt Atherton knew something about orphans. He certainly knew about death. But, damnit, he knew about life too. Or, at least, he intended to.

He felt the pressure again, and vertigo. He gripped the door, opened and shut his eyes a few times, tried to focus on the kid on the bicycle across the street until the double vision passed. The woman at the register stared, called out to him.

But he just pushed the door open and got the hell out of there.

AVENGE ME

THE GIRL IN THE TANGERINE kimono walked barefoot down a path of aquamarine tile along a shadowy corridor. Her eyes glowed in the dimness, the coronas of suns blazing on her contact lenses. With her every blink, solar flares twitched along her corneas, and track lighting responded by perking up a few lumens while the blowers from the air conditioning vents went silent. She smiled. Perfect teeth.

The hall curved away before two large rooms. On her right, an expansive kitchen extended past a mahogany and chrome monstrosity of culinary engineering, sporting deep stainless steel sinks and an eight-burner stovetop that put out enough blue heat to make an East Coast chef drool on his double-breasted spun-poly. She sashayed just within the door, briefly glancing the other direction, toward the darkened living area, before proceeding inside. Her smile slipped only a smidge at the faint buzz of snoring coming from a leather sectional.

The refrigerator. Ah. She pulled the steel door open and revealed rows upon rows of fresh greens and reds and yellows. Frothy and cooling juices occupied plastic containers in the slot along the door. She let go of the handle and lifted a large cherry wood cutting board from a blue marble countertop, tapping it on the side and watching dried powders and herbs and assorted paraphernalia float down to the ceramic. She ripped towels from a roll and seized a large triangle of a knife from its holder to add to her ensemble.

Lastly, she pulled a warty knob of a fruit from one of the bins, a flesh-colored number that almost seemed to wriggle and pulse with blood circulating under its thin skin. Star-shaped nibs sprouted from its surface like blackheads. The girl clenched it against her chest and sank her thumbnail inside. She pulled her thumb out and sucked on it softly as she made her way toward the couches and the large screen monitor that occupied an entire wall of the living area. The flavor zinged along her tongue and down her throat, and she shivered at the effect.

The suns on her eyes shimmied again and the wall screen blinked into electronic life, throwing up the numbers 0228 in the center along with a vertical bar for VOLUME that had been muted. Under her gaze, the level climbed into the red and, with a sly grin and nip at her bottom lip, she brought the speakers roaring into life.

"AW YEAH!" a baritone drawled, the speakers quaking the walls.

"Oh my fucking God!" screeched a young girl on the couch below her. The girl in the tangerine kimono perched neatly beside her, her mouth twisted into a smirk.

The barrage of a vacation package vid occupied the full screen. Champagne in fluted glasses bubbled, and glassware came together in a clink; slot machines whirled and chanted sweet sounds of another winner. Over a jazzy score, the same smooth baritone cooed, *"Paradisa Atlantia, baby. What ARE you waiting for?"*

A naked young man tumbled from a stuffed lounge chair across the room, his bony ass smacking hard on the tile. He got up with a snarl; greasy dreadlocks swarmed about his face like blond serpents. "Asshole!" he shouted. But the girl in the tangerine kimono only shrugged and took up a position near the arm of the now-vacated sectional. She dismissed him with a brief flitter of her fingers, the sculpted nails gleaming like pearls.

The younger girl hovered, a comforter wrapped around her shoulders barely covering her small breasts. Inked pink roses and dark vines snaked around her nipples. The rank fabric of the comforter set the air awhirl with a mixture of musk, marijuana and sweat. Damp crimson panties twisted around one of her ankles. The man stalked over, and she leaned into the tat-riddled flesh of his shoulder. His chiseled body and face had already started the characteristic wither of the Peel freak. Below the waist, the ravages of self-abuse and mutilation—the girl in the tangerine kimono fought back a guffaw.

His menacing posture was evidently all for show. The girl in the tangerine kimono merely crossed her legs and fixed her gaze on another advertisement. This one was for shoes, nothing but straps and ridiculous stiletto heels. For a lark, she brought the knife up to her face and waggled it; she sized-up one of the man's pectoral muscles as if looking for a place to make an incision. Then she narrowed her eyes and indicated the hallway behind them with a jerk of her chin.

Bleary-eyed and beaten, the man took the blanketed wastrel by the hand and retreated from the room. As they neared the master bedroom, an older man poked his head out. He gave the couple a curious glance, then stepped into a pair of butter-soft slippers and rubbed his palm across a whiskered jowl before ushering them inside. His hand floated to the back of his leathery neck as he began his own trek toward the living area, his steps those of a suddenly-penitent school boy.

∞

The Ringmaster tilted his head a bit for the magic touch-up of his tanned skin when yet another gofer burst through the door. "BP! Got the tallies for ya!" He thrust a handheld to the tip of his boss' nose.

A few swipes at the device and the Ringmaster got at the significant figures. The numbers weren't bad, but they weren't where they should have been. Not on his program. Not on *his* stage. "When are they going to do something about the Left Coast?" he roared. "We're absolutely getting *killed* out there."

"Sir? Page hits, downloads? Don't you see it, BP? You're at the top again!" the toady groveled.

"Top of what?" The Ringmaster waved away the brushes and suckers working the excess powder off of him. "The late night broadcasts? Don't you *dare* compare me to those *talk show* asses!" He charged out of the chair, slapping at the silk, braying for all the life in him. "There's going to be some changes around here, damnit! I'll not allow, I'll not ACCEPT, I'll not TOLERATE, *slippage* of any kind! This, this, is an unbelievable—OUTRAGE!" He slammed the handheld into a nearby trashcan and then gave the can a kick across the room. He advanced on the cowering minion, hands flexing, until the youth skittered out the door.

The Ringmaster knew. This was his electronic circus, and he'd been at the top of the game for eight years running. Even before that, he'd outworked and outhustled all his contemporaries, including the old war horses that others deemed out of his league. Untouchable, they'd said, but the Ringmaster had proved the experts wrong. He knew this business of American entertainment inside and out.

So no one—none of these hollow-eyed, saddle-shoed, wrinkled-khaki, dirty-kneed, six-months-and-gone producer motherfuckers—was going to tell him the kid they'd corralled for tonight's festivities wasn't a potential show killer.

Just one look at him told you everything: he was *soft*. How had he gotten booked? What the hell were the agent, the manager, the handlers—what could they have been thinking? No one could give him a straight answer. Backstage in the Green Room, trying to open up a conversation around a heaping pile of pieced fruit, the Ringmaster noted not only that the little brat was almost glued to his mama's side (at age 22!), but that he'd also selected a banana to eat. Out of the myriad of organically-grown produce to choose, he opted for the sweetest, softest, *gushiest* thing he could get. Spoke volumes right there.

It curdled the stomach. Oh, this boy was deadly. And as if things couldn't be worse, they'd slotted him to lead off. First segment! The lead quarter hour bombs, that's it. Dead show.

"Come on, Bert, five minutes now," oozed the producer. "Nothing to fret, old boy. Just remember, trust in the hooks. The hooks work. And once it's sold, go in for the jugular. Plunge it in. Hooks and blades, baby, hooks and blades."

Gah! And the name of this kid. Corny! It was laughable. Yet the younger crowd ate up the boy's "songs". He crooned the most insipid lyrics and watched as articles of teen princess clothing took to the air and landed at his feet. *Sign my panties, Clive, sign my pushup training bra . . .*

"Work it, Bert. You're a pro!" another moron spouted. *Can they hear themselves when they blabber on like this? Do they believe their own pap? Do they know whose butt they are kissing? King of the goddamned NET. I invented the hooks. I can use the knife better than anyone still alive to play in this game.*

Little things the kid had said earlier now bugged the hell out of the Ringmaster. He'd kept talking about *opportunity.* Well, hell, they all did that, but he'd looked a little shifty when he'd said it, like something Freudian was trying to barrel out from his maw. *Rebirth. Moving in a new direction.* "You mean like, taking up acting?" "No, no, nothing like that—" *Be more of an inspiration. Challenge people's perceptions.* "Politics?" *Motivate . . .*

They'd talked about the gimmick. Giving the consent, the nod, thumbs up sign, like a Roman patrician from an old black-and-white silent movie, sitting in for Emperor Bacchanalius or whoever, lying back on his sofa bed. But only at the correct time, only at the Ringmaster's request, only at the peak. And finally, the giant red and gold switch. All the Celebrity Q's wanted to touch it, so that wasn't unusual. They loved to throw it back, make a joke, feign electrocution, bulge eyes, grit teeth. This kid wasn't having any of that, though. He'd just stood there, staring at it without a word. When an assistant had offered a demonstration, he'd shaken his head and quickly moved away.

Or am I just imagining things?

The part that really got to him, though—the thing that he kept seeing in his mind, over and over—was at the end of their little conversation, before the kid latched back on to mama. "It's gonna get crazy out there tonight, Mr. Pavo," he'd spewed out through bites of the fruit. "I'm gonna put it all out there. Really give them something to think about!" And then that little twist of his lip, near where you could tell he'd had some metal garnishment at a time before he decided to swim in the middle of the show-business river. "They'll be talking about this one for years!" The kid wouldn't look him in the eye as he pumped his hand and pulled away in a rush.

They'd vetted this punk. No Amnesty International; no Human Rights Watch; no United Nations/Geneva summit-cum-laude graduate. Not even a whiff of PETA, save the dolphins, save the Siberian tigers. *I mean, hadn't they?* He tried to picture someone in the brain trust who might not have his best interests at heart. Who could the traitor be? *Et tu, Simon Munoz, executive producer?* But—down that nightmare path loomed madness. He had to let it go.

He brought his hands down, snapped his cuffs, cupped his fingers then worked the collar. Don't touch the coiffure, the woman—Cynthia? Paris?—she'd nailed that back in dressing. He swished his tongue around his lips, blinked, and began the breathing exercises. Taking the beat down. Hooks and knives, yes. But no chains, baby.

"Break those chains, hoss," someone said. "Three minutes, Bert."

If that little shit tried anything—*breath, hold, hold, hold, exhale, long, longer . . .*

∞

The prisoner made a half-hearted stab at a steak on his plate, but all he was doing was moving things around. His fork tines burrowed into the meat, but the subsequent knife jab didn't cut, and the prisoner made no attempt to saw at the flesh.

"Oh, Lee," a fat guard named Dolan said softly, watching the act from across the small table. "You're gonna break my heart, aren't ya?" He tilted a black cap back on his head and gave Lee a half-grimace.

Lee looked up at Dolan with hooded eyes and commenced pushing the loaded baked potato around, whipped butter and sour cream spilling from the sides. His wrists were free of the handcuffs while he ate, but his ankles were shackled, and he kept shifting in the stiff new uniform he sported: a lemon-colored coverall with no collar and half-sleeves. He looked like he hadn't slept in days

The two men weren't alone. Standing behind the guard were more official personnel: a man and woman, hard and primed for a fight. Both had their batons in hand and the woman packed a stun gun. Above them, multiple cameras shifted and whirred. There were more devices, a lot more. Lee had seen them as they'd ushered him down the hallway. His every move was monitored. Broadcast for, how many pairs of eyes? That picture—of a million blinking red-rimmed lids and dark matted lashes—disturbed him suddenly. He trembled and took a deep breath.

"Come on, Lee," Dolan said. "You gonna eat that thing? It's a filet, bro. Conner did his best piece of cooking on that." He grinned, revealing a partial he clicked with his tongue.

Lee pushed the plate forward and shook his head. "Nah," he said, placing his cutlery on the table with care, watching the black cudgels as he did it. He leaned back in his chair as far as his bonds would let him go.

"Now, Lee. You best enjoy it, son," Dolan said with a wink. "Conner put his damn foot in it." He eyed the dessert plate that just touched the entrée. "Especially the pie. Dang, that looks like a good'un." He flicked a thumb at the whipped topping, and pulled back a dollop. He lapped it off with his tongue.

Lee shook his head. They'd shorn his blond hair away like a new recruit's at a military boot camp. "I watched this old boy on the vids last Tuesday," he said softly, placing his hands on his chest. "Real big guy, six-five or something, about 250 pounds. Texan, I think."

"Uh-huh. I remember that one."

"He was doing all right at first. They brought him in the room, the one they do all that kind of work in. They've used it before, I seen it. Anyway, this fella is doing pretty good until they have him sit down and start laying these straps and belts across him. And damned if he didn't lose it then. Started crying. Goddamn. Starts to begging, praying. Calling out for Jesus. I couldn't believe it. He'd been playing such a hardass all the way up until they were going to hit him with that heat, and he just came unglued."

The guard shook his head. "Not sure about that cream on top," he said. "Lemon meringue or chocolate silk, I get that. But on a nut pie? Don't make no sense, does it?"

Lee continued. "That beam they hit him with. Some kind of microwave or laser or something. You could see it working on him, Dolan, burning that skin, slow, until he was brown as a French fry at the bottom of the pan."

Dolan spun the pie plate a half turn. He reached for the fork, and used it to dust a flake off the crust. "You sure you can't eat even a bite of this?"

Lee brought his chair down suddenly with a bang, and the two other guards sprang forward, their clubs raised. But Lee only brought his elbows onto the table, and put both hands around to the back of his head, massaging his neck. "It wouldn't stay down. And I'm not going to mess myself. Not today."

The guards relaxed, and Dolan cut into the dessert. He put a forkful in his mouth and chewed deliberately, then sent it down with a swig from Lee's nearby ale. "What I want to know," he chirred, "is what kind of pecans they put in here. Georgia paper shells? Or MoKan northerns? There is a difference."

Lee flicked at his nose with an index finger, looking at the gray wall on his right. No window. No carvings or inked obscenities. Just a smooth layer of interior paint. Not even any brush strokes to unveil the work of a state employee just going through the motions. "This other, maybe a month ago, he gets up in that room, and before they do one thing, he up and blows chunks all over himself."

He lowered his voice. "Shit himself, too. They put it all on there, Dolan. They don't cut nothing out. He stood there like that until they peppered him with looked like birdshot from a thousand shotguns from all directions. Probably bigger, ball bearings or something. Didn't even look like a person when they finished with him. I kept staring at that mess and thinking, 'not me, not me. I ain't going out like that.' I'm gonna look straight ahead and whatever they do, whatever they decide to finish me off with, I'm gonna face it. I'm gonna shut my mouth tight, keep my eyes open, stand up straight, and let them know just who I am."

Dolan's lips were smeared with topping and brown syrup at the edges. "Well, that's one way to do it," he finally said with a belch. "Not many a man can go to meet his Maker like that nowadays. Not good for the ratings, probably. But you do that, Lee. Somebody out there might appreciate it."

∞

"Baby?"

The old man stopped a few feet short of the sectional. The belt of his black velvet robe had pulled loose. The robe fluttered open, and he had to work the sash around to cover himself. He glanced back at his bedroom, as if in search of moral support, but neither of his houseguests had reappeared in the hall.

Flashes of thunder and gunshots flared from the vid speakers. The still photograph of an automobile froze in the center of the screen, and the camera slowly zoomed toward the backseat, showing the bare legs of a prone female, and the black and red blood trailing from the scene.

"Innocent life—taken!" roared an off-screen narrator. "Another family—shattered! Left in the wake of unspeakable acts of cruelty, DEPRAVITY. A world ever more dangerous—until all of that changed . . ."

"*America's Got Justice!*" A presto of trumpet peppered through a roaring baseline of drums, shaking the theater speakers against the walls. "Where you, America, will see JUSTICE SERVED . . . and cast your vote in HOW WE DO IT!"

More bass, and the martial themes of the program, the driving pound of drums and fifes, were like a sonic wave, driving the old man backward two steps.

"Dedicated to our men and women in law enforcement—who put their lives on the line every day. And to those people we will never forget. The victims of the most heinous of crimes . . . MURDER!"

A blizzard of photographs flipped across the screen. The people they featured were young and mostly female. Glamour shots, like they were from the pages of high school and college yearbooks.

The old man cleared his throat. "Sweetheart, why are you watching that?" he tried to coo, before coughing up a catch in his throat. "Please come back to bed. Our guests . . . don't be rude . . . "

The girl in the tangerine kimono stuck a middle finger in the air and twisted her hand left and right in a lewd fashion, her gaze never leaving the carnage on the screen.

"Here's your host . . . Bert . . . PAVO!"

∞

The Ringmaster took two steps up to the stage and nodded at the audience applause as he high-stepped to his mark. He knew just how tight to hold the smile, when to let it give, when to take the modest bow, how to hold his hands in a prayer-esque gesture. He truly fed on the adoration, manufactured though it almost always was. Yet there was something about the live audiences, especially the young ones, that made him feel not unlike a vampire, and he subtly poked his tongue tip to one of his canine teeth. *Milk it, just a little, just a wee bit more . . .*

He didn't kid himself. They were the high school and college masses here on Spring Break, number one, and number two, they were here to see the three guests the producers had lined up. The more he'd run it through his mind, the more he decided that putting the boy up first was a master stroke. Best that Bert have a go at him while he was at his strongest, and deflect any weirdness with his own wit, turn the interview to his advantage. If they'd saved the boy until the end—the Ringmaster wasn't sure he'd be able to parry any political ambush and keep it from becoming fodder for the night's web chatter and the morrow's coffee talk.

"My goodness! You are amazing!" he crowed, and the audience response was another splash of tonic for his energy level. Most hosts would have been distracted by the bouncing flesh, making lame jokes and laughing loud, killing the mood. But not The Ringmaster. "I guess you all know what week it is, am I right?" More war cries from the frat boy contingent, and girlish screeches from the bleach blonde honeys. "Yes, it's Celebrity Q Week here at *America's Got Justice*. And I gotta tell you, as much as we like doing each and every show, all year long, there is just SOMETHING SPECIAL about Celebrity Q Week. Am I right?"

The response was seismic, and he could picture the buffoons in suits tucked away somewhere, nodding in appreciation at what he brought to their table: ducats. Yuan, Euros—the tattered remains of the American dollar. Maybe one or two of them had at one time or another privately carped about the premise, the morality of turning death into spectacle. But he was Bert Pavo, damnit, he was The Ringmaster. And, at his core, he could really give a shit.

"Then what are we waiting for?" he bellowed, holding two beats on the last word, opening his eyes wide, maniacally. "Let's bring out our . . . FIRST . . . CELEBRITY . . . Q! This young man hails from RIGHT HERE IN MIAMI, F-L-A! Here to perform AMERICA'S . . . CURRENT . . . NUMBER ONE HIT SONG . . . introducing . . . CLIVE . . . . CISCO!" The boy's last name rolled off his tongue, and he held onto the vowels right into the music. *Cleeeve Seeeesco*. The kid, on cue, strode to the center of the stage and soon had the audience waving their arms and singing in time.

To a fucking ballad!

The Ringmaster sat in one of the flimsy beach chairs arranged nearby and took in the lad's act, mystified. The teenyboppers, the college crowd, the soon-to-be-boxed-in cubicle worker monkeys—they adored him. This was a song for their Age. Cisco was their poet, their Dylan. Was it even appropriate to the occasion, on a program like this? How the hell did he know? Not that it mattered. He'd have the Pope on the show if he could get enough page hits from all the fish-eating masses and put a few cardinals' butts in the chairs. He fantasized about it for a bit. Getting an audience with the pontiff. The corresponding website hits made him swoon.

Halfway in, he lost the gist of Cisco's song lyrics. Something about a *handjob* from beyond the grave, maybe? No, couldn't be. But the boy had the performing chops, no question. This was his moment, and he was taking full advantage of it. There was a little of the old Pavo in him.

"For miles I feel the emptiness,
Alone, desire your unseen caress,
These midnights of complete stillness,
Please reach for me, paranormal girl . . ."

The Ringmaster had to give the lad some credit. His writers knew their stuff, judging by the audience's reaction. And the kid could really sell it. He had the pipes to deliver the pabulum. He hit his octave limit, straining and wincing from the effort, then with eyes open to the night sky, implored an act of telekinesis be produced from the heavens, and he wasn't taking no for an answer. Looking out at the crowd, the Ringmaster noted by the expressions of scores of the young people nuzzling the stage that Cisco could have gotten that service any time he wanted.

It came back to him again. The memory, the Green Room. Cisco actually asked him how they were going to do it, the execution. Most Q's didn't want to know. And it was right there in the contract, the method was held secret until the very moment of truth. No one had ever asked him directly right before they were to go on. But Cisco wanted to know. And if that wasn't a declaration of intentions, what was?

Is it you, Durban Kiltie, senior producer? Are you with the men behind the curtain, taking my boot measurements while you adjust that dagger you just shoved into my back?

∞

The guards escorted the prisoner through a maze of corridors and stairs. At last before them was a single white metal door without windows. Lee noted that it had no blemish on its painted surface, either. There was a flat handle instead of a knob, and just above that on the wall a single steady yellow light beamed. Dolan mumbled something unintelligible into an intercom, and the crew waited.

Lee coughed, and followed with a heavy breath. "Dolan, I—" he said, before swallowing and blinking his eyes three times quickly.

Dolan nodded, put a hand on Lee's shoulder and gave it a soft pat. They'd reattached the prisoner's plastic wrist restraints and Dolan made sure they were secure and comfortable. "I know, Lee. I know," he said.

"The truth. I need to tell it. So somebody knows," he continued hoarsely.

"Shh, it's all right, boy," Dolan answered. "You do what you need to do."

"I didn't kill that girl," Lee began, staring hard at the guard, but Dolan didn't look up from his work. He'd knelt to the floor and snapped another restraint to connect the others. Lee fixated on the crown of the cap, shifted his belted wrists a smidge. The two guards behind Dolan both had their stunners out and activated, seemingly daring him to try an escape, their lupine glares boring into him.

Dolan rose, making his knees do all the work. He looked into the prisoner's face, and the corners of his mouth eased up into a confident smile. "No?" he asked, slapping at the legs of his work pants. "No, I don't guess you did. But then—why are we here?"

Lee seemed surprised by the guard's response, and paused a moment.

"I was there—"

"Oh, that's right," Dolan interjected easily. "You just witnessed a murder, but you didn't have anything to do with it."

"No," Lee said, eyes shifting away from the guard's steady gaze. "I didn't see—"

"Of course not. Because who wants to see something like that? A young girl, barely out of elementary school, being ravaged, tortured." Dolan shook one of his wrists, and the joint creaked audibly.

Lee looked down, at his manacles, at the floor tiles waxed smooth and shining.

"You were there, but it was—who?" Dolan continued. "Your brother? Your half-brother? A cousin. Somebody you had to protect. Somebody you still are protecting. You wouldn't go through with this if it was just one of your drinking buddies. Ain't that right, Lee?"

Lee took a quick breath, shuddered, raised his chin a bit to look at Dolan and back to the floor.

"I've heard this before, Lee," the guard said. "I know this story by heart. And it's always the same. I've never escorted a guilty man down these halls."

Dolan noticed the light begin to pulse, and put his hand on the prisoner's back to guide him into position. "All that horror—it's like a bad dream," he said. "We want so bad for that to be all it is. But wanting that ain't going to change anything. The dead stay dead. That baby ain't coming back to save you. No, sir."

Lee lifted his foot, testing the tethers that bound his legs. The last thing he wanted was to do a face plant in front of millions of people. "I didn't want nobody to save me, Dolan," he said after a moment. "I just wanted you to hear me out. You've been good to me, every day I been here. I just wanted you—I know you don't believe the story. I just wanted you to believe me. That's all."

"I believe you, son," Dolan replied, giving his shoulder another squeeze. "I always do. Every time I hear it."

They watched the blinking light. All of their breathing had quickened in the silence, or so it seemed to Lee. They were a team, he thought. A unit. And he was the most important one in the group. He was the one with the ball, looking for the goal line. The one everybody had come to see. He gave his head a shake, thrust his head and shoulders back, and tensed, and waited.

∞

"You think you're such hot shit, but without me, you'd be out on the goddamn street!" *Bullshit.*

"I'm not going to let you keep treating me like, like garbage! I'm better than this—" *Uh huh.*

"I'm a child? You're the child! You haven't done half the living I've done!" *You're that old, gramps.*

"My money! I'll be damned if I let you spend one more dime of it!" *Blah blah blah.*

"You know where the door is!" *Yawn.*

She had the fruit pinned to the cutting board with the flat of her hand. It bled as she ripped it with the knife. The song on the vid was ending, and she whispered the final lyrics as she worked, rarely looking up. Bert Pavo was saying something about a world tour: Istanbul, Algiers, Caracas. She smiled each time the young entertainer responded. His voice rose as he talked about the people he had met, and about the sights he had seen. She lifted her gaze back to the screen as one of his answers seemed particularly interesting, exuberant, and she watched as the camera focused on his bright eyes, his neatly-thinned eyebrows, his smooth and full lips, his glistening white smile.

Caracas. The girl in the tangerine kimono had been there. Modeling on a South American tour. Sao Paulo. Rio. Santiago. Buenos Aires. She remembered all the young faces. Such happy people, waving banners, shouting encouragement, singing their love songs, chanting their slogans. Beautiful people.

Cisco had been there, too. He'd been so much fun, cutting up and making everyone feel at ease. They were shooting some vid on a pristine beach. Los Roques Archipelago. He'd been at one of her fashion shows, and invited her to come out for the day, make a little extra money. She'd been hesitant to lose one of her few days off, but he truly was persuasive, in his way. Charming, with not a touch of the smarm that was part of her everyday existence. And he could be so exuberant, especially when talking about the news of the day, in some far off country. He wanted to change the world.

The month had gone by much too fast. Everything was speeding by. Life. It made her dizzy sometimes, thinking about where she was going, what she was going to do next. How she would get there, who would accompany her, who would love her.

Anywhere, any way, with anyone she wanted.

She touched her cheek, slid a finger slowly past her chin. She felt for a blemish. An old habit. This had been a problem area in her early teens, but not anymore. She knew she would find nothing but the soft, smooth skin she was blessed with, in tandem with the best creations of dermatological science. Now and forever.

The knife made short work of the outer peel, and she severed one of the knobs neatly, sighing softly. She lifted the piece to her mouth and drank from its oozing, sucking the juice until it filled her mouth, and let her teeth rake across the bruised flesh. She murmured contentedly. *Los Roques*.

∞

"One thing—the thing that I most got out of it, was that people out there are, are the same as we are. We're all people, and we all want the same things. And we, we need to realize that, and realize just how important life is. And cherish it. And fight for it." Cisco's eyes were getting a little wilder the further he climbed out onto the conversational limb. The Ringmaster let him go on, nodding, so patient. "We've got to stop the pain we do to others. I think that's what I take from all I've seen on the road. Meeting so many different people and their various cultures. But knowing that deep down, there's that decency, in all of us. We have to focus on that. Life—all life. It's—precious."

The Ringmaster placed the fingertips of each of his hands together and rubbed them easily. "Well, what a tremendous opportunity you've had. It just sounds like something you'll remember for the rest of your life, Clive. And what a beautiful message to share with us tonight. Life is precious. I want to introduce you, and our audience tonight, to someone who so loved life. Someone who shared the same thoughts that you've told us about tonight. She had an amazing personality, and intelligence, and a compassion, Clive, unlike anything I've ever seen in a child so young. This girl had such spirit, and a beauty both inside and out. Let's watch."

The montage opened with photographs of a baby with shiny dark eyes, a winning toothless grin. These were followed by stills of a toddler astride a unicorn, wandering around a kitchen tableau. Next it switched to video. The girl had a spoon, and popped it smartly against the lid of a pan. This was shortly followed by amateur video clips of a young brunette dancing and singing. She was maybe eight years old.

Cisco shifted in his seat. The Ringmaster knew the boy thought he'd gotten an important message delivered to the world. But just like that, like smoke, it was disappearing. Blown away by a child who now lifted her chin and lip-synced to a voice that was unmistakable.

Cisco leaned forward, on the edge of his chair. It looked like he wanted to vault up, wave his arms, stop the proceedings. But his chance had come and gone; the power had shifted, and he had to sit there, frozen, and watch helplessly. It was Pavo time.

The video progressed. The girl was now 11 or 12. She chattered more. She wore a t-shirt that bore an image that was, again, unmistakable. She looked into the recording device, announcing that she'd gotten the tickets to a concert, starring her favorite performer. She was going with her parents and her friends. She was an organizer of the local fan club at her school. The montage shifted, showing a mother, a father, sisters. Happy scenes from birthday parties, from holidays. Gifts unwrapped, excited shouts. That face again, that innocent, happy, face.

Yes. There was an art to it. Of the thousands of victims they had to choose from, they knew what buttered the proverbial bread. No shots of the broken sidewalks, the trash-lined gutters that filled so many American neighborhoods. No graffiti-smeared walls hiding the grey and lifeless interstate highways that droned endlessly. No boarded up windows, no aimless youth jumping down grimy front steps while their grandparents crouched behind bolted doors, gripping their baseball bats and 9 mm handguns. No, these were the manicured gardens, the palisades. Not a hair out of place on these kids. No bruises pocked their little arms and legs. *And the stuff the research department can unearth to match up with our honored guests . . .*

At last, Cisco slid back in his seat. No camera recorded that. Only the Ringmaster noticed. The lad's face was a tangle of multiple emotions. He brought the back of a hand to his mouth, pressed his lips to it. The girl in the video sang again, her voice that of an older girl. Unpolished, but still with the charm of any child that had no idea how she sounds, but sings with such earnestness, eager to get every lyric right. Every one of *his* lyrics.

And just at that moment, they froze the girl's image, and it softly faded as they segued into a shot of the mother, no longer a party bystander, but front and center with her grief. Distraught, on a witness stand in a courtroom, tearfully recounting the worst night of her life. They watched her come apart, undone by the realities of what had become of her daughter. Then the father at a press conference, begging for the life of his missing child, by this time already mercifully dead. "Just let her come home," he wept. "Just let me bring her home." An imposing man in the party videos, he appeared to be bent almost in half, a Quasimodo in a wrinkled plaid shirt and faded jeans. Unwashed hair, jaw covered with stubble. He stepped away from the makeshift podium awkwardly, and the two young girls with him, the sisters, dropped back with frightened faces, before vanishing like spirits.

∞

Lee stood before the door. His legs shook, and Dolan tightened his grip on the prisoner's shoulder. He grunted, coughed a little, and turned to the guard. "It's gonna sound crazy. So, so goddamn crazy, Dolan," he said. "Stuff popping into my mind. Weird random shit."

Dolan smiled, nodding. He stared at the blinking light, awaiting some command from the button in his ear.

"I'm—I'm back in high school," he said. "I'm still in cross country, with the team. And we're out doing our road work. Out on this two-lane asphalt road. 32 highway. Coach Benton, he'd driven it in his truck so he knew exactly how far we had to go and then turn around and haul ass back to the school.

"And so you'd be running along this road, and it was fall and still pretty hot, and up you'd go, and then you were on this overpass. Right over an interstate, and you could hear the cars passing underneath you. Tires just hissing on the road, like they were frying in the sun, too."

Dolan didn't say anything, but his smile tightened.

"And when we got to the middle of the overpass, we had to cut across this stone median in the center of the road and start back to the school. Weeds were growing up in it, but we'd kind of beat it down with our shoes, had a nice patch to hop over and get going the other way. But sometimes—" he hesitated. "Sometimes I'd stop and go to the edge and look out over that highway. You'd see all these trucks, all these cars, heading off somewhere. And the air would change, and that wind coming up, blowing in your face, felt so good, you didn't want to go back. Maybe—maybe you'd want to jump down. Hit one of them cars. Or drop down into one of those trucks. Like they do in the movies. You know?"

Dolan nodded. "That's right, Lee."

"But one thing I never did. I mean never, and it wasn't a big deal then, but it just popped into my head right now. I never kept going to see what was across that overpass. On down that road."

Dolan patted his shoulder. "I've been over there, Lee," he said. "You didn't miss nothing."

"You did? How—?"

"Oh yeah, I been on that side," Dolan continued. "Our coach would make us run miles, too. Especially if we were late to football practice. Yeah, I saw that side of the overpass. More than I wanted to, some days. He was a goddamned sadist."

All four of them were quiet. Dolan watched the light and listened to the static and hiss from the electronic button in his ear.

Lee looked at Dolan. His lower lip had started to tremble as much as his legs.

"Nothing on that side but more of the same," Dolan said.

The light's flashing slowed, and became a steady gleam again. A locking mechanism clicked, and the door before them swung open.

"Go on, now," Dolan said, like a stage whisper. "They'll tell you what they want you to do, inside."

Lee shuffled into a brightly lit room. He could barely lift his feet in the restraints. As he moved, he heard the door close softly behind him.

∞

She bit deeper into the fruit, the tart flesh splashing inside her mouth. She could stand it no more and grabbed the larger bulk of it, unpeeled, and placed the wound to her lips. Then she bit, and the juice burst from the gash she'd made, splashing from her lips down her chin and neck, onto the tangerine kimono. And still she bit deeper, shuddering as her body reacted to the flavor, gulping what rushed into her throat as fast as she could. She gasped and sat back, her mouth once more twisting into a smirk, and felt the soft cushions of the sectional through the fabric pressing to her back. She sighed, then held the carcass against her chest and curled her body around it, shivering.

∞

Cisco watched the vids to the end and was silent, vanquished. No more about Istanbul. Nothing about the wonderful and vibrant culture of Brazil and their people so full of the esprit vivre. The image of the girl was frozen on the vid. The hidden microphones across the viewing area, amongst the crowd, picked up the sobs, and the rage.

"So full of life. A beautiful young girl," the Ringmaster pronounced sadly. "Wasn't she, ladies and gentlemen?" The roar of applause then, deafening. He stood up from his chair. Cisco pressed his head back past the top of his chair, his eyelids tight. Was that water creeping from the corners of those lids? The Ringmaster thought. *How do you like my hooks?* He left the boy, walking steadily to the front of the stage, his arms at his sides. Even before he reached the edge, he could hear the cries and murmurs in the crowd begin to coalesce. The chant was halfway where he wanted it before he'd even raised his arms. Oh yeah. The birds were ready to feed.

"Who knows what she could have accomplished in this great country of ours? But we'll never know. Her family will never know anything more than the pain they still feel today. You can be sure of that." The chant was clear. Three words, the name of the most popular webcast in the world, picked up and joined by every voice in the crowd. The Ringmaster lifted his arms deliberately, keeping his mouth a straight line across his face as he lifted his chin higher, his eyes open wider.

"What about it, America? Do we deserve some JUSTICE?" Another roar, with more of the crowd joining in. He moved his arms even higher, as if he could feel the energy, the electricity churning out of them, entering him. "A GRAND JURY thought we did! A jury of twelve thought we did! A court magistrate thought we did!" He shook his hands and looked up into the night sky. There were stars there, but he couldn't see them from all the brilliance of the Klieg lights that burned around him. "We don't need to read a coroner's report! We don't need autopsy photos. We don't need to see a vid of a crime scene!

"Clive Cisco! You are our CELEBRITY Q!" He whirled around, his right palm out in front of him, beseeching. "How about it, Clive?" He rolled his shoulders back, widened his eyes as he slid forward in time to the words the audience continued to scream to the heavens. "America wants Justice! America needs Justice! AMERICA DEMANDS JUSTICE!"

∞

The woman's voice guided him to the center of a large empty room. Her tone was soothing and easy. He guessed no one else could hear the voice, certainly none of the millions of viewers across the globe who watched him. She was only for him, and he took his place as she directed.

He stared up at the ceiling, and saw his own reflection on the mirrored tiles. Leroy Kenrick Malone. He still thought the new uniform was ridiculous. But it was show business. He had a part to play and he couldn't mess this up, no matter what. He would not disgrace himself. He was a man and he'd show them how a real man died. He gave them a solemn face, one at peace with whatever had been decided. And then the ceiling tiles slid away.

Above him gleamed an array of lights so intense he couldn't help but wince. They would understand. It was like trying to look at the sun; only there were thousands of them. Burning little suns. He felt the heat above him. And then he realized the lights were reflections on metal. Thousands of blades, like teeth that now moved, rotated, picked up speed. And the sound of the churning as they lowered drowned out any scream that tried to burst from his throat.

WHATEVER IT TAKES

MERLE EDGERS PUSHED UP HARD against the shatter-proof glass enclosing the catwalk and pressed his palms against the bleary surface like he wanted to grind flesh from bone.

"This Regency operation of yours, it's a—what? Execution agency, right?" the ChemStar CEO had asked him seconds earlier in front of the Director of Prison Manufactures for the state of California, assorted businesspeople, and San Jacinto Penitentiary's warden. The CEO's face was pursed like he smelled something foul. *"You think you can handle a real business, make an actual—well, product?"*

Remembering the man's smirk, Edgers jammed a hand into the pocket of his suit jacket. He gripped the sample-sized can of ChemMist the CEO had tossed his way. His fingers itched to whip out the can and blind the ChemStar prick with a blast of chemical spray—a *product* of the man's own company, there was a laugh for you.

Forty feet below, on San Jacinto's factory floor, inmates in crimson jumpsuits tended the production line, mixing a highly toxic pesticide with inert powders. Ten feet along the catwalk, the Director chatted and joshed with the ChemStar honcho while a bevy of men and women—the presidents of other, less notable competitors—jostled around them.

Edgers heard none of that conversation. Instead, in his head, he replayed the Chemstar bigshot's final comment to him: *"Can't blame you for wanting to move up into prison manufacturing. I just hope you can handle the sharks. And the regs. What was the name of your little prison start-up? PMS?"* Plenty of laughter.

"PPS," Edgers muttered now, to himself, through clenched teeth. Progressive Prison Systems, which the dickwad-in-a-fancy-suit damn well knew. The Director had made introductions all the way around before starting the tour. Edgers' jaw silently popped, a painful shifting at the mandible like a bone bursting in and out of joint.

If he was scared of a challenge, he wouldn't be standing on this damn catwalk with some sneering corporate exec he needed to outbid. PPS was only doing penny ante jobs right now, running meat processing operations in two small state prisons back east. This contract—for a factory in a soon-to-be-built penitentiary north of San Francisco—would be huge, and Edgers was determined to win it. If he couldn't gin up for competition with a few sharks, he'd have been a plumber like his dad, crawling in the muck under busted-up sinks and sticking his hand down plugged toilets, standing ankle-deep in liquefied shit when a sewer line broke—(Edgers' pack of school friends witnessed that one and made shit jokes for years)— living in a suffocating apartment where vids flickered and yapped twenty-four hours a day and the wife stumbled through at midnight wearing her beige Zippee-Mart apron. Edgers' dad: never once promoted from the bottom rung, and too stupid to even recognize the insult.

Edgers glowered down through the glass. The San Jacinto facility was one of California's most productive, which was why Miss Bureaucrat had dragged the heads of the bidding companies on this tour. Sacramento wanted even greater productivity from the next project "while not sacrificing the punitive element the inmates have earned and the public expects," as the Director phrased it.

The inmates toiling below were all men, mostly in their twenties or thirties, with the pallid look of underground creatures. Even the black guys somehow managed to look pale. No way to tell how many of them might be Executables, the kind of lowlife murderers and rapists that victims' families contracted with companies like Regency to kill after release. For a nice fee, of course. All legal, all above-board, but still—not that he ever would have admitted this to anyone—the execution business carried a slightly slimy feel to it, an oiliness that reminded Edgers of earlier days in his working life. Not so much standing in shit, but later, when he was with the cartel and everything wasn't exactly legal.

His mouth was dry and he wished he had a little scotch—just a swallow or two or three—to wet it. He shook his head. He *was* legal now. A businessman who'd started Regency from nothing and turned it into one of the top five execution companies in the U.S. And, Jesus, if Mr. ChemStar thought Edgers didn't know about pains-in-the-ass, the guy needed to meet some of the killers in the Regency stable; you couldn't find a more high-maintenance, over-weening flock of divas.

"Mr. Edgers?" The Director motioned for him to follow the others who were clanging down the metal stairs at the end of the catwalk. "Thanks for coming today. We'll look forward to seeing your bid."

Edgers forced a glad-hand and a grin. Yeah, the Director was interested in the bid—and the gratuity expected to accompany it. All part of the cost of doing business the way the big boys did it.

The ChemStar CEO was in the lead—*big man, packed schedule and every item on it oh-so-vital*—striding down the gray corridor after the warden, heading toward the parking lot without so much as a glance back at Edgers or the others. Sneering mouth, well-cut suit on a tall frame. Looked so comfortable, so at ease, like he'd had the whole damn company—the whole executive lifestyle—slipped to him on a platter.

Well, the bastard didn't know a shark—Progressive Prison Systems, yeah, *PPS*—was about to slice right through his territory. Edgers twisted a malicious grin at the man's back and plunged toward the cab still waiting where he'd left it three hours ago. The flask had better be right where he'd stashed it.

The driver slouched behind the wheel, eyes closed, bleached blonde dreadlocks flowing over the headrest. Edgers slung himself into the back, eyed the driver through the glass partition for a second or two, then turned his head to one side and spat onto the asphalt. A few years packaging insecticides in San Jacinto would clean this guy up in a hurry. First thing to go would be the mangy braids.

Anyway. He longed to get back to the hotel, grab his luggage, hightail it to the airport and get the hell out of California. There were a lot of freaks back in Philly, but nobody could hold a candle to California.

His comm buzzed.

Edgers grabbed the flask he'd discreetly tucked into the elastic pocket on the back of the driver's seat and took a long swallow. He squeezed his eyes shut. Thank God. Three hours with nothing but a coffee pot and a water cooler in the prison's 'hospitality' room had left him feeling dehydrated. The scotch would take care of that.

He answered the comm.

A 3-D holo of Geoff Whelk's flabby amphibian face squatted on the small screen. Jeez, the guy was really packing on the pounds. He'd been practically cadaverous back in the day.

Edgers smacked the partition. A small square slid open in the glass. "Hey," Edgers snapped. "Back to the hotel." The dreadlocks shivered and withdrew. The empty square in the glass closed. Tires hissed across pavement.

Edgers sank back and frowned at the holo. Whelk regarded him in return. A problem, undoubtedly. Wasn't it always?

"Yeah?" Edgers said. "What can I do for you, Geoff?"

"We have a bit of a snafu, Merle."

Edgers screwed up his eyes for a moment, considered whether Whelk would think it was suspicious if he ducked out of vid range for just a few more seconds with the flask. He longed to feel the fire trailing down his throat.

"We? Or you?"

"Oh, most definitely 'we'."

Merle glanced back at the penitentiary's high walls, the razor wire shredding the air. If—*when*--PPS took off in a big way, he would seriously consider selling off Regency Executions. Get rid of the whole mess.

The folds of Whelk's neck wobbled and sank into position again. He was smiling, but a vulpine sharpness came into his eyes. "You'll recall that I just completed a particularly tricky job."

Edgers dug into his memory and realized with a small shock that, in fact, he did *not* remember the recent assignment schedule of this man, the first hitter he'd hired and one whose years of success had qualified him for the most lucrative execution contracts.

His gaze slid to the black screw cap and silver neck protruding from behind the elastic. The rectangular shape of the flask itself plumped out the pocket, hinting at the liquid it held, teasing him. A coldness fizzed from his scalp down through his chest. Maybe the flask and its many cousins were the reason he couldn't remember—which frightened him, but not so much that his mouth didn't want to suck at that silver neck.

Instead, he crammed a rectangle of gum into his mouth, jawed it, said "Yeah, yeah, and?" as if he remembered every detail but didn't have time to delve in too deeply.

"I sent in my substantiation this morning. The Executable's DNA was confirmed. There's no question that I harvested the right man and in the way the contract specified."

"Ah, yes, that was—"

"—garroting. Just what the Executable himself was convicted of doing to *his* victim."

"Right, garroting, DNA, okay, so what's the problem?"

"The problem, Merle, is that I just spoke with that manager you've installed at the San Diego office—"

A surge of panic before Edgers was able to dredge up the manager's name. "Brendan Roth." The panic loosened its grip.

"Indeed. And Mr. Roth informed me that my bonus payment out of his office would be delayed."

Edgers frowned at this. "Did he say why?"

"No. Only that the money would be in my account within five business days."

"What the hell?"

"He informed me that all payments through his office were temporarily delayed, on your say-so."

Edgers swayed forward. "I never authorized that."

"Well, I thought not, Merle. I told that young whelp there couldn't possibly be cash flow problems, not when business has been so robust. He was quite rude. I don't know where you scooped him up from."

Edgers waved a hand, distracted by the thoughts churning at his brain. "He's got the business background, Ivy League, all that."

"If one considers Dartmouth Ivy League."

"You've obviously done a little research." Edgers' hand snaked toward the flask. He bent forward for a moment, like he was tying a shoelace, and managed a hasty swallow. He thrust himself back into vid range. Eighty-proof ignited every blood vessel.

"Perhaps you might have a chat with young Master Dartmouth," Whelk said. "Make certain he understands how we do things at Regency."

What the hell *was* Brendan Roth up to? "I can do better than a chat," Edgers said. "How about a surprise visit?"

Whelk's eyebrows mooned upward with unconvincing surprise. "Oh, are you in sunny California at the moment?"

"I'll get back with you as soon as I've talked to the guy."

"Excellent. I'll expect the full amount in my account today." Whelk's holo vanished.

Edgers rapped the partition and gave the driver the change in destination, then angled himself closer to the side window. The penitentiary had vanished behind dusty red hills. They were approaching civilization again, if you wanted to call it that, with the security lanes to the highway only a mile off now. Taco stands and pop-up burger joints fringed the road, with misspelled signs and grimy counters he imagined to be seething with salmonella and e. coli. Skinwaste hookers in stilettos reeled on the crumbling pavement of motel parking lots. Rust-eaten trucks, their parts cannibalized, stared from the scrubby flats like some kind of grotesque American-style sphinxes.

His wife kept talking about how they should relocate out of the U.S. entirely, head to Chile or Hong Kong, somewhere safer, with a better standard of living. Maybe she wasn't entirely crazy. They lived in a secured neighborhood, one of the best in the Philadelphia area, but you couldn't squirrel yourself away behind gates and guards every second of your life. And when you came out, the skinwastes and beggars were all over the damned place, more of them every day it seemed like.

Thirty minutes later—ID chips checked, car searched, fee paid—the cab cruised the highway's left lane. Dense metallic fencing caged the road, arching in from both right and left like a nightmare version of a French boulevard.

Edgers sat upright, muscles tensed. He gripped his comm in one hand and brought up the San Diego office's accounts for the past six months. He studied the records with an almost ferocious concentration, but saw nothing unusual.

Next he brought up Regency's employee file on Brendan Roth. A holo of Roth quivered above the screen. *Young whelp.* Yeah, Geoff wasn't half-wrong about that.

The kid—Edgers couldn't help thinking of him as a kid—was six-foot-three with the physique and the easy white grin and sun-bleached hair of someone who'd spent his life around regattas and lacrosse fields. St. Michael's prep in Connecticut, then Dartmouth—yeah, *that* was probably the tragedy of Roth's teenage self, getting the kiss-off from Harvard and Princeton—and then straight to Wall Street, courtesy of Daddy's extensive contacts in the financial sector.

And then? A stumble. Hell, a staggering fall onto his knees.

Edgers had never understood the specifics. Wall Street wheelers and dealers did things with investment products that, in his opinion, no one really comprehended, including themselves. The firm for which Brendan worked packaged and promoted some suspect holdings that quickly soured. Losses were enormous and the one SEC official who apparently hadn't been bought off came sniffing around. Bottom line: the firm shoveled the full shit-load of blame onto Brendan and a couple of other kids. Brendan was temporarily toxic on Wall Street and when Brendan's father had hinted that his son might make an excellent addition to Edgers' staff, Edgers had been quick to agree.

Mr. William Roth. Brendan's father, with a Yale law degree in addition to banking experience, had investments in both execution agencies and prison factories. He and Edgers had bumped up against one another over the years thanks to Edgers' stellar rise in the executions industry and now his start-up in prison manufacturing. William Roth's upbringing wasn't hardscrabble-and-bootstraps, but it wasn't as soft as Brendan's either. The two men respected one another's success. It was a professional friendship Edgers took pains to encourage. Mr. Roth's current position with the DOJ boded well for PPS's growth. Having Brendan as a Regency employee was like having a fifth ace in the deck.

If Brendan hadn't had connections, Edgers wouldn't have given him the time of day. Edgers preferred to hire people who'd come up the way he himself had, from nothing. Those were the people with daring and intelligence, driven not only to achieve money, recognition and respect, but also driven to do anything to keep from tumbling back into the pit. Fire burned so hard in their bellies that their stomachs should've been smoking.

"Stop here." While the cab pulled over, Edgers snatched up his flask, drained the contents, and tossed the empty container onto the floor. The cab stopped a block down from the Regency office. Edgers paid the exorbitant fare, shoved the door open, and stepped onto the sidewalk. The cab slid away.

He hadn't been to the west coast office in person for six months. Which, he reflected now, was negligent. Stupid. He prided himself on having a handle on every aspect of his businesses, but the bigger the businesses got, the more unwieldy they became and the less he could keep track of all the customers, all the employees, all the small parts that needed to work together harmoniously to make the profit line sing.

The office was located near the waterfront in one of the few remaining sections of the city that had any prestige. He'd made sure not to go cheap on rental space. Well-heeled clients didn't want to wade through syringes and shell casings to get to an appointment. Still, the area looked seedier than he remembered. More storefronts were empty, 'for lease' signs bleating failure from otherwise blank windows. A brown slime of disintegrating garbage gathered around the bottom of the trash can at the street corner and bled from its gaping mouth. Not as much pedestrian traffic as he expected, and the people he did see moved swiftly, a determined jut to their shoulders like they just wanted to get their business done and get out.

When he reached the office, he loitered outside its bay window. The front desk was empty, the reception area devoid of people. A good time to slip inside. He moved swiftly and as quietly as possible through the entry space, but not so swiftly that he failed to notice the room's aura of sterile poverty.

Where a heavy oak desk once imposed on the room there was now a wood-laminate table with spindly, foldable legs, little more than an upscale card table. The plush leather sofa and chairs were missing too, replaced by what appeared to be lumpy cast-offs with ugly orange and green upholstery. Pale squares of empty space decorated the walls instead of paintings.

There were similar squares on the walls of the corridor leading to the back offices. Each missing painting sparked a new combustion in Edgers' gut. The scotch he'd guzzled before exiting the cab blazed up in his stomach like pure gasoline.

He'd shot big bucks not only on the lease but on an interior decorator with instructions to buy whatever was necessary to give the place a look of solid, trustworthy respectability. A cross between a bank and a funeral home. A business that grieving, angry people, still mourning the murders of their loved ones, would know they could trust to destroy the murderers upon their release from prison. The fees Regency charged were substantial. Customers had to feel confident transferring those kind of funds, had to feel comfortable signing the legal contracts. Had to know, instantly, that they weren't handing their business over to some fly-by-night outfit, but to professionals.

So why the hell did the place look like some kind of shyster easy-loan set-up?

A pair of voices chatted in one of the offices he passed. The door was closed. A man laughed. A shining, silver, easy laugh that grated on Edgers' nerves and that he recognized as Brendan's.

The other office doors were open. Edgers swerved into each doorway, one after the next. This place was supposed to have, what, four staff besides Brendan and the receptionist? So where was everybody? Taking a five-hour lunch break?

He'd give them a break, all right. Break their butts when they hit the sidewalk after he canned every last one of them.

He stepped into the offices, one by one. Like the reception area, they now had cheap furniture, no decorations. The high end processing units and screens were gone. Instead, off-brand equipment squatted on the desktops.

In the last office on the right, a can of cola sweated onto the laminate table beside a balled-up fast food wrapper. Jesus, these people couldn't even toss their trash all of twelve inches into a wastebasket? And what the hell was that? A lighter, a spoon and ... Edgers stumped across to the desk, leaned down to examine a silver smear that curved across the surface like the glittery trail of some magical species of snail.

It better not be what he thought it was.

He dabbed a fingertip into the substance and flicked his tongue against it. His tongue went briefly numb, then prickled to extravagant life, tasting an impossible sweetness.

Synth. He was paying some asshole to sit here and do synth.

And Brendan was letting them get away with it. Or, hell, maybe he was doing it too. Maybe he'd been dabbling in this shit back on Wall Street. Maybe that was the real reason they'd tossed Mr. Ivy League on his ass and nobody would look at his resume.

The last room on the left was a combination storage room/cleaning closet. Back behind the mop and the bucket and the spray bottles of glass cleaner and the 24-packs of toilet paper stood an elegant chair upholstered in finely-grained leather. It glowed the mellow color of brandy. Edgers stepped closer, stared at it. Stared past it at a painting he recognized immediately. A Scandinavian seascape by an up-and-coming Swedish artist. The interior decorator had convinced him that it was not only high-class décor for the office, but an investment for the company as well.

And now here it sat in its fifteen-thousand-dollar frame, waiting for—shit, it was pretty obvious now, wasn't it? Waiting for whatever buyer Brendan had lined up to come finalize the purchase. The proceeds of which would undoubtedly go into Brendan's silk-lined pocket.

Edgers' hands shook. He opened and closed his fingers, hard, wanting to grip something, someone. Wanting to snap the bones in somebody's arm, crush somebody's throat. Listen to them suck for air.

He backed out of the storage room.

Get control. Get control get control GET control.

The bathroom was next to the synthfreak's office. He shut himself in, hunched over the sink, ran icy water over his wrists and slapped it against his face. It dripped from his chin, splattered the front of his pale blue shirt with dark spots.

Breathe.

Breathe.

Don't act without thinking first. That's what dumb thugs stuck down in the pit do. Not the guys at the top.

Edgers cupped his hands under the faucet and scooped up a mouthful of cold water. It didn't burn a clean path through his brain the way a straight-up whiskey could, but it would have to do for now. Should've worn a jacket, something he could conceal a flask underneath.

He grabbed a fistful of paper towels and shoved them over his shirt front, wiped his face. Strands of black hair rollercoastered around his forehead. Slamming the used towels into the trash, he shouldered the door aside and bulled his way down the hall to the room where he'd heard the laughter.

He pushed the door so hard it ricocheted off the stopper on the adjacent wall.

Brendan, leaning easily against the front edge of his desk, jolted upright. The woman beside him stuttered backwards, her stilettos machine-gunning the carpet with tiny holes. He remembered her, vaguely. The receptionist—Heather something-or-other—but she hadn't looked so skeletal and leathery-brown six-months ago.

"Oh. Hey. Hey!" Brendan rearranged his expression from chagrined surprise to hearty chumminess as he clambered forward, grasped for Edgers' hand, gave it an energetic pump. Edgers kept his own hand limp, a dead thing, and was pleased to see fine lines of anxiety shred the younger man's forehead. Otherwise Brendan looked the same, toned physique, halo of golden hair, and all. Damned if the guy didn't manage to carry the faint, cool tang of New England salt air on his skin.

Brendan finally let Edgers' hand drop. "Awesome to see you, Mr. Edgers. You should've let me know you were coming. We just finished lunch."

Edgers regarded the receptionist. "I bet you did."

"Uh, Heather?" Brendan ticked his head toward the door and made a *chk chk* noise with his tongue, as if he were guiding a horse.

Heather scuttled in the direction indicated. Her long legs were stork-thin, knobby at the knees. Edgers wondered if she'd chosen the blouse with its full, long sleeves to hide injection marks on her arms. Her jittery air, eyeballs skittering in their sockets, green-bean muscles: everything pointed to a synth habit, and a bad one. One arm trailed back like a broken wing to pull the door shut behind her.

Brendan glanced at a clock on his desk. "We could still go get a coffee." He grinned with those perfect white teeth of his. Just a good ol' boy with 50 grand of orthodontia. Edgers hadn't been able to afford that kind of dental work until he was in his 30's and just the sight of it brought up the froth of his anger again.

"Or even a beer if you didn't mind a little alcohol on work-time," Brendan added. That conspiratorial grin again. "Just one, of course."

Edgers was president of two companies. Brendan Roth was nothing but a regional manager for one of them. No need for a coffee klatch. No need for a trip to the pub, even if the thought of a cold foamy beer worked at his saliva.

No need for niceties.

Edgers stepped forward. He was almost as tall as Brendan and, with his chest pushed out, felt satisfactorily large and threatening. The kid better be pissing his pants right about now.

"So tell me what's going on," Edgers said.

It was obvious from the momentary sideways cut of Brendan's gaze that he knew exactly what Edgers was talking about. But he kept that bright, clean expression on his face like he was some kind of professor's pet, sitting in the front row of a classroom, certain that in due course an 'A' would appear on his grade report.

"Well, business has been good—as I'm sure you know—and I just reeled in a couple of really great jobs earlier this week. Excellent bonuses attached, for the hitters assigned to them and for the agency, both."

"Profitable, huh?"

"You bet."

"As profitable as selling off every item in this place, piece by piece?"

Puzzled updrawing of eyebrows. Quick quirk of the mouth, as if not sure whether to take the question seriously or not. "I'm not sure I follow."

"You really need to get the buzzer at the front door fixed, Brendan, because I had time to take the full tour before you even knew I was here."

"Oh." A phony dawning of comprehension on Brendan's face. "Okay. You mean the stuff in the back?"

"The stuff?" Edgers couldn't wait to fire this punk. Spread his bad name all over the industry. Snuffing out a man's career prospects was not all that different from snuffing out the man himself. "The furniture and artwork and equipment I paid a small fortune to buy for this place? Is that the 'stuff' you're referring to?"

"We've moved everything temporarily. Spring cleaning, you know? Just in August." Breezy. God, Edgers hated breeziness. Rich, slick people thinking they could get away with anything. "The cleaning people asked us to take things down to a minimum so they could really do a thorough job. It'll all be back to normal next—"

"Geoff Whelk called. Said you were postponing payment on the job he just finished. For which he is owed the bonus immediately."

"Oh, yeah, that was just—"

"You told him it was on my say-so."

Brendan had that puzzled look back in place as he shook his head. "He must have misunderstood."

Edgers let the words fly. "You're out of here, Roth." Imagined the words plowing like bullets right thought the guy's left ventricle, ripping up the aorta.

Frozen befuddlement. "Mr. Edgers? I don't think you understand."

"I understand everything."

Brendan had been leaning back against his desk again. Now he pulled himself upright and dropped the befuddlement. The angles of Brendan's face—square jaw and high cheekbones—were blades.

"No, Mr. Edgers, you really don't."

"Find a box. Get your things together."

Instead, Brendan went around his desk and sat in the chair behind it. This chair, Edgers noticed, was the original one he'd bought for the office: thick, ergonomic, leathery heaven. Edgers had a similar model from the same Taiwanese manufacturer back in the Philly HQ. That was the problem, wasn't it? You spoil an already spoiled brat with nice equipment and

they take it for granted. He'd like to see this brat—
whelp—start a business from scratch, scrabble around
for seed money, doing whatever it took, *whatever* it
took—risking the cops, risking prison, risking a slow
death at the hands of assorted drug thugs and slingers.
Doing it all with no top-drawer connections and no
fancy education.

"You have ten minutes," Edgers said. "And that's
being damn generous of me."

Brendan just leaned back in his chair. "My dad's not
going to be happy. Things might not go so smoothly for
PPS. You don't want to hurt your new business before
it even gets off the ground."

"Your dad's already seen you screw up and get
yourself canned for some esoteric crap of a crime he
probably only halfway understood. This? Siphoning off
money that's supposed to go to the hitters' accounts on
the day of the kill? Selling the damn lamps and desks
out from under me? Nothing hard to understand about
that kind of theft. Your dad'll understand why you had
to go. Don't kid yourself."

Brendan actually put his feet up on the desk, the
Italian-worked leather loafers gleaming in the halo cast
by the lamp. He laced his fingers behind his head.

Edgers leaned forward over the desk, his hands
spread against the surface, his fingers surging with
blood and ready to wrap around the kid's neck.
Whatever it takes.

"But what about when I contact Dad's friend,"
Brendan said, smiling, actually *smiling*. "You know, the
California attorney general? And I tell him about
Sergei?"

Edgers didn't move. Blood throbbed at the back of his eyeballs. Sergei. Fuck. The hitters in Regency's stable were divas and some of them—Sergei, for one—were getting maybe a little wild, a little out of control.

Brendan grinned. Not so much as one filling silvered up the perfect white molars. "Yeah. You know all about him, don't you? Those jobs he did up in northern Cali last winter. The one in Oregon. Talk about violating federal regs right and left."

Edgers drew back from the desk. A burning afflicted his stomach, burping up periodically from his esophagus. "Which you didn't call him on, did you, Regional Manager?" Edgers pointed out, sounding calm and controlled, but with a bad feeling like he was sliding down a steep incline and the earth and rocks around him were sliding too. "Compliance with the regs in the western region is part of your job."

"You're the company president. You've been getting reports about this kind of thing since—well, since before I was even with Regency. Everybody knows you've been letting hitters break the rules."

"Bend."

"Break."

Edgers was silent.

Brendan suddenly let his feet drop to the floor. The thump sounded heavy and solid. Final. "So," he said, "all in all, I don't think you'll want to let me go."

The rage that smashed through Edgers was hurricane-force. A tsunami in the blood that roared across his brain, made it hard to think clearly. "You—"

"Ahh." Brendan actually tutted an index finger at him. At *him*, the boss, the president of the company.

Like the punk thought he could get away with anything, anything at all.

Brendan blazed that white smile and said: "We could still get that beer if you want. No?" Shrugging, he fished around behind his desk, brought up a bottle of vodka and a single cut-crystal lowball glass. Brendan poured two fingers of liquor into the glass, took a drink—raising one eyebrow at Edgers as he did so—and relaxed back into the chair.

Edgers couldn't speak. His tongue wormed against his teeth as if applying a little pressure might start a miraculous flow of vodka. A high-pitched hum sang in his ears—the sound of his own blood. Blood pumped down the heavy muscles of his arms, threatened to burst the vessels bulging from the back of each fist.

Every nerve in his body urged him to barrel forward, grab the kid, squeeze until the kid's vertebrae cracked and his windpipe crumpled like gift wrap from an abandoned Christmas present. The muscles in his hands remembered the motions. He'd done this before, and could do it again, right now.

His mind flashed on the ChemStar CEO. Top guys like that—the business execs running the show--didn't crawl around, letting their emotions whip them this way and that.

Get control.

But the kid's going to bleed me, he silently protested, his fists tightening, eager to do their work. *And he knows it. That's why he's got that fucking monkey grin on his face.*

It started with the furniture, the artwork, the office equipment, siphoning a little money from the accounts. It ended—where? A spigot tapped directly into

Regency's main accounts? Why not insist on access to PPS's accounts too? And a top level job with PPS as it outgrew Regency? How about president and owner of the whole damn enterprise? Nothing too good for a Dartmouth man.

Just get control of yourself.

Edgers lurched to the door, slung himself down the hall and back through the lobby. Heather shriveled against the back of her chair like a strip of beef jerky with glistening eyeballs stuck to its front. She gaped at him.

Edgers' throat was so parched it hurt to swallow. To hell with beer. He needed something stronger. Plenty of bars and clubs down by the waterfront. He thudded that direction.

Slices of gray Pacific water appeared, visible between buildings, sloshing uselessly in the harbor. Signs above doors and windows: Ernie's Pub, Margarita Cantina. He could see his future the way that damn Roth kid must envision it, the two of them entwined forever, Brendan dragging him down, down, endlessly down.

Edgers bulked forward along the sidewalk, his shoulders battering the mild air. He hadn't busted his ass building Regency just to watch some leech, a fucking *bedbug* suck the blood right out of it.

He stepped into The Green Olive. He ordered a scotch on the rocks, sat in a booth by a window, and stared outside. The wind had picked up. It shoved against the waves, slapped them, drove them forward like they suddenly had somewhere to get to in a hurry.

A waitress brought the drink. He downed it in one swallow and motioned for another.

Once Edgers had raised enough money to start Regency, he'd sworn that there'd be no more illegalities, at least not of the bloody, brutal, unrespectable sort. Because if a man wanted the governor asking for his advice on the jobs situation someday, wanted to lounge around fancy political receptions with CEOs and power brokers and influential donors and tell those people how things were going to be . . . well, you had to be a particular kind of businessman for that. The kind who used loopholes and lobbyists, not guns.

But if some spoiled rich kid forced his hand? Nobody could just expect an ambitious entrepreneur like himself to plunk down in the middle of the road and let some brat run him over and wreck his American dream.

Whatever it takes.

Edgers had an entire stable of lethal employees working for him at Regency, but he couldn't use them for this job. Better that no one knew about this one.

The waitress set another glass on the table. Edgers drank this one slowly, savoring the mellow warmth, the wetness on his tongue. The way it soothed every raw nerve and calmed the interior storm. Clarified his thoughts, helped him see that, yes, just like any of Fortune's 'World 500' top executives, Edgers was making the rational, necessary, difficult decisions to improve productivity and profitability.

The quick efficient pleasure of hearing bones snap, the shutting off of superior monkey grins had nothing to do with this.

So. How to do it? He rummaged through mental images of kill scenes his Regency staff had sent him over the years. Simple gunshots, stabbings, machetes, strangulations, drownings, poisons, incinerations.

His thoughts stopped at that last. A good cleansing fire to purge the cockroaches. Yes.

He motioned to the waitress, pointed to the shelves of bottles glittering behind the bar. "I'd like to buy a couple of those."

The waitress glanced over her shoulder, then looked back at him, her forehead puckered. "I don't know . . . "

"Whiskey," he clarified, squinting at the bottles, checking the brands, gauging how much liquid he'd need to douse Brendan thoroughly. "You sell Mountain Lion? Is that the 150 proof?"

"Yeah."

"I'll take two bottles. No, three."

"We usually only sell by the glass. We're only licensed to—"

Edgers pulled his mouth into a grin, turned his palms up. "I'd really appreciate it. I've got a party to go to and I need a—what d'you call it? Hostess gift."

The bartender swung his head up from the tumblers he was polishing with a cloth. "It's okay, Brenda." He nodded, grinned back at Edgers. "Nothing wrong with moving a little product."

Moments later, the waitress placed three bottles in a row in front of Edgers. She flapped a couple of plastic sacks down beside them. "To help you carry them," she said.

"Oh, I'll manage. Thanks."

He reached in his jacket pocket, felt the three-inch can of ChemMist lodged against the seam.

Perfect. First the Mist. Then the Mountain Lion. Then the lighter. He didn't have one, didn't smoke, but the office synthfreak sure did.

And that office. They'd turned it into a shithole anyway, in a rotting part of town. This way, he might be able to move Regency to a different space without breaking a lease. And who knows? After it all went down, he'd let things settle, sure, but he'd need a new office manager, wouldn't he? And since he had every intention of winning the prison factory bid, PPS would be looking to add some real go-getters to its staff as well. He'd tell Spence, back at Regency HQ in Philly, to get him contact info for some of ChemStar's top performers. Edgers might just have a little headhunting to do.

He took out his comm, buzzed Brendan's personal line. Smiled when the kid answered.

"Yeah, hey, Brendan. I've been thinking." Edgers kept his voice deferential. A maid asking if she might be permitted to move Mr. Roth's slippers from beside the bed in order to vacuum the carpet. "How about we get that drink, after all?" Blood flooded dark and muscular through Edgers' hands. "Sure, I can push my flight back. No problem."

Roth cut off the connection. Edgers pocketed the comm, leaned back, took a drink. Studied his hands hard against the tumbler, the way his fingers followed its curve and squeezed the sweaty glass.

Dartmouth didn't stand a chance.

CLAY

THE THING ABOUT THESE YOUNG GUYS, the ones just coming into the business, is they were hard. Like flint, granite, and marble put together.

And Clay Dedrick, half-a-dozen years past the big five-oh, felt about as hard as a bar of wet soap these days. It was obvious that the young hitter standing outside the door of the motel room saw him that way. Old, soft, and falling apart.

The kid had one corner of his mouth tucked up into his cheek while his stare, cool and black, took no more than two seconds to appraise Clay before sliding away. Behind him, the sky was dead and flat, bits of sleet driving down like nails. Frigid gusts of air cut to the bone.

Clay wavered in the doorway, one hand gripping the frame. He should pull himself up straight and tall, and relax his hand, but he couldn't do it. Or, at any rate, couldn't seem to summon the energy to force himself to do it.

"You're Alec," he said, knowing as he spoke that he should have waited, made the other guy talk first. Except that this guy—this Alec Garity—looked like he could outwait the Apocalypse.

The young man nodded and continued to gaze past Clay into the room.

Clay glanced uneasily over his shoulder. The room had already looked pretty bleak when he'd first cracked the door the previous afternoon and the cigarette burns that annihilated random bits of carpet were the work of a previous occupant, but he still had to admit that his brief residence here hadn't exactly improved the real estate. Empty bottles and fast food containers pimpled with bubbles of dried cheese cluttered the top of the dresser and nightstand. The bed's rumpled sheets were a dirty shade somewhere between beige and gray, and long iron strands of Clay's hair coiled against the pillowcases.

He looked at Garity again. Garity was tall and lean, cleanly-shaved, his jeans fresh and his insulated vest brilliantly blue.

"It's a crummy motel," Clay said, offering an apologetic shrug even though he knew he shouldn't. "But you can't exactly expect the Ritz in a town like this."

Garity didn't respond.

Clay waved a hand toward the Crescent Moon Motel's cratered parking lot and the neon sign on its far side. "Yeah, pretty lousy." The sign's dingy sliver of moon throbbed above a burned-out heart the color of long-expired meat.

"Anyway." He lowered his arm, shuffled back a step. "I've got the extra key for you over on the dresser."

"No, thanks."

Already halfway to the dresser, Clay stopped. "So you do talk."

"If there's anything worth saying." It figured. Garity's voice was deep and resonant, powerful but not too loud. Controlled.

What did it feel like to have control of yourself, your life? Of anything at all? Clay was damned if he could remember.

"So." Clay paused. He stood midway between door and dresser, shifting his weight from foot to foot and trying to figure out what to do with his hands. "The office book you a solo room?"

"I've got a room a couple of towns over."

"Really." Since when did HQ book two hitters, assigned to the same job, into different hotels? "Nice place?"

"Not bad."

Jeez, did the guy not like to talk or did he just assume old, fading-out Clay wasn't worth the effort?

And had Garity booked the other hotel himself or did the office think the guy deserved better than what they were willing to shell out for Clay?

Clay decided he wouldn't mind a beer. Or two.

It took four steps to reach the cooler on the floor beside the bathroom door.

Yeah, the bathroom. He saw it through Garity's eyes, the door wide open, yellow lightbulbs buzzing over the vanity, damp washcloths heaped on the floor and a hand towel hanging over the edge of the tub like a dead snake. Wadded clumps of toilet paper and Kleenex were mounded at the top of the wastebasket. A faint odor of mold clung to the tiles and pushed itself out into the bedroom. The smell of decay and dead things. Faint, but able to make the gorge rise if a person let himself pay attention to it.

Clay shoved the bathroom door shut. The light still buzzed on the other side, pressing its dismal yellow illumination through the inch-wide crack between door and carpet.

Kneeling, he tugged the lid off the cooler. Half-a-dozen bottles nestled in the slushy ice. He saw this through Garity's eyes too, and knew it didn't look good: old guy crouching over a beer stash in a seedy motel when there was a job early the next morning.

But, hell, tomorrow was tomorrow and there was plenty of time for the beer to work itself through and out of his system.

And, to be blunt about it, Clay didn't much care at this particular moment how it—how *he*—looked. He didn't even care, not really, if the job went off okay. He just wished that the client had requested a quick, clean kill, a bullet to the head. Fast, easy, and over with. But no. It couldn't be anything that simple. The client had specified a long, elaborate, and extremely detailed plan for the Executable's death, all of which was to be streamed, real-time, to the client. Cheating was not an option.

The E was scheduled for release from the penitentiary at 7:00 am and Clay had serious doubts if he and Garity combined would be able to make their way through the client-provided torture-and-death bullet list by noon.

He pulled out a bottle, twisted the cap. Cold vapor rose like a ghost from the bottle's lip. Looking up from where he swayed on his haunches, he said, "You want one?"

"I don't drink."

Of course not. "Before a job?"

"Ever."

Clay had to put his free hand against the desk to help himself stand. A quick pain burned through his right knee. It was always there now, every time he had to stoop down or kneel. Arthritis, he supposed. Maybe he was going to need a knee replacement. Which, frankly, was another thing he just didn't want to have to mess with.

Sometimes it seemed like that's all life was . . . an endless string of things he didn't want to deal with.

He stayed upright only long enough to head to one of the room's two blocky, uncomfortable chairs and collapse onto it. He took a long pull from the bottle. Maybe, if he drank enough of it, it would give him a shove, push him away from this feeling that everything was gray, the same, and there wasn't much point to doing a damn thing.

"You're letting the cold in." He waved his bottle at Garity who still stood in the doorway. "Why don't you have a seat?"

Garity shook his head, briefly, no motion wasted. "I'm going to head to my hotel."

Clay stared at him. "We need to go over to the site, do the recon before dark." He glanced past Garity at the sleet. Barely 3:00 and the low gray clouds were already darkening with the approach of evening.

"I already did all that."

"When?"

"This morning."

Clay slouched deeper into his chair, took another drink, and saluted Garity with the bottle. "Well, thanks for letting your partner know." It seemed like something he should say, Clay thought, even though, to be honest, he was glad that someone else was dealing with the legwork. Although, per Regency Executions' policy, each hitter on the team was required to do recon for every job. No riding a more diligent hitter's coattails.

"Merle may have assigned us to the same job," Garity said, "but I don't do partners."

"No, no, me neither," Clay answered and realized it was true. He'd done hits with just about every other killer on Regency's staff over the years, but there wasn't one he'd consider a partner, much less a friend.

He spent a lot of time alone. He'd lived on his own since Lucy left him and took the kids all those years ago. Not even a pet dog or cat. He thought about returning to his apartment tomorrow night after the long kill session and the clean-up, with the paperwork completed and sent in to officially fulfill the contract, every 't' crossed, every 'i' dotted. A half-empty jug of souring OJ in the fridge and dirty laundry waiting on the closet floor. Another thought crossed his mind: so, don't go back. Go . . . where? Anywhere. What did it matter?

"Looks like it's going to be a long job," he said, just for something to say.

"That's why I'm calling it an early night," Garity answered. "See you out there at 0600." He started to leave, paused, glanced at the cooler. "If you make it."

Frosted gravel crunched under Garity's boots as he crossed to his truck. He hadn't bothered shutting the door to the room so now Clay would have to make the effort. Clay pushed his hands against the armrests, forcing his bulk up out of the chair. From the doorway, he watched the glow of taillights on Garity's truck, turning out of the lot onto the narrow two-lane highway that, in this ridiculous 20-mph stretch, formed the main street of this flea-bitten dump of a town.

Clay shivered. The sleet was intensifying, the wind blowing harder. The caulking around the window was bad and the plastic blinds rattled at every gust of wind. He stepped back and shoved the door closed, flipping the bolt in place. Not much in the way of security, but it's not like anyone was looking for him.

He returned to his chair and to his bottle, soon supplanted by bottles number two and three. He flicked on the screen. Twin vidstreams flashed silent images of two soccer matches: Mexico City 3, San Diego 2; Dallas 4, San Salvador 1. Clay didn't care about soccer, never had, but he turned up the volume on the San Diego game and tried to concentrate on what the announcers were saying.

Which was the usual. So-and-so was having a stellar season, but this-and-that was out with a torn ACL. Million dollar contracts with bonuses that made his own look like coffee money. Good-looking girls in short shorts jumping around on the sidelines, a vision which moved Clay's loins not at all. Apparently that part of him was as prematurely dead as the rest.

Around the time he polished off bottle number three, his gut started to ache. Sharp pains like the pinpricks of tiny needles jabbed at the inside of his stomach. He'd first noticed this early in the summer. In the beginning, it only happened when he was deeply into his cups, but now the pain attacked even when he'd downed nothing but a lightweight's serving of 3.2. He hadn't seen any blood—yet—but he wondered if he had some ulcer action to go along with the ruined knee.

He thought of the caps in his travel bag, shiny red-coated pills of the finest synth. He'd been carrying them around in an old man's seven-day pill case for months now, his backup for the day his stomach lining could no longer handle so much as a single beer or when he just needed something . . . more.

The caps offered the prospect of a brief out, an escape, along with the near certainty of addiction. Despite the many stringy-muscled, blank-eyed synthfreaks he'd witnessed over his career, it wasn't fear of addiction that had kept him from sliding a cap or two down his throat. No, it was the fear that even a drug reputed to give a high more intense than any other pharmaceutical wouldn't be able to penetrate his listless spirit, his shellacked brain.

And once you understand that even synth can't give you a momentary jolt of life, then what do you do? What else is there?

The chair was hard. But he sat there until pins-and-needles attacked his thighs. Then he retreated to the bed, but the mattress was soft, a rectangle of marshmallow fluff that made his back ache. So he hoisted himself out of the bed and stood in the middle of the room, his face screwed tight as if his stomach was full of paper cuts and his knee sliced down the middle by a razor.

He stood there for a good ten minutes, his arms tight across his chest. He was shivering even though the door was closed. The blinds shuddered with the wind. When he went over to see if he might be able to use the cord to somehow lash them into place, he saw that a thin frost covered the window both inside and out.

He laid a palm against the radiator just beneath. Cold air blasted from the icy metal vents. The room had no functioning thermostat, just the blower control and the hotter/colder dial set into the top of the radiator.

Well, the blower was working. That was one thing functioning in this shithole HQ had seen fit to stick him in. But no heat. With the night sinking toward a predicted ten degrees, he couldn't just hunker down and ignore this.

Irritation snapped briefly into his mind and he grabbed it and refused to let go. Irritation was almost as good as a drunken fog or a chemical euphoria. It was, at least, something rather than nothing.

He dropped onto the edge of the bed and thumbed the button of the comm unit on the nightstand.

The comm's tiny cracked screen flickered with an image of the same tiny, cluttered front desk where he'd checked in the day before, but with a different clerk behind it. Yesterday's had been a doughy white guy who was either deaf or pretending to be. Today's was a Spanish-looking girl, equally doughy, her jaws in constant motion as she brutalized a wad of gum between her teeth.

"Yeah?" she asked. No accent, just the same flat Midwestern nothingness of intonation that Clay himself had. No eye contact. She was busy with something—probably her own personal comm— behind the counter.

"I'm room 124. The heat's stopped working."

The clerk didn't say anything for a minute, just jawed her gum a few times. "Wow, it's supposed to get really cold tonight."

Another flicker of irritation flashed through him, but was immediately smothered by a wave of exhaustion. He just did not want to deal with this. "Exactly," he made himself say. "And that would be the problem."

"Hunh." The girl's eyes were still directed at something below the counter. "Well, I can call the maintenance guy and see if he can get over here today."

Clay thought of the rubble-pit of a parking lot and the condition of the motel's neon sign and was not surprised to hear there was no maintenance person on site.

"By 'today', you mean this afternoon?" he asked. And good—there it was again, a sliver of emotion passing through him, a pinprick of resentment at this girl's stupidity that forced him into a Q&A.

"Well, Luis works for a couple of apartments too. And some other places on the side. So he's pretty busy." The girl's gaze flicked up, snagged for an instant on what must have been the image of Clay on the screen on her work desk, then dropped right down below the counter again. No, there wasn't much about Clay to attract the lingering attention of the young ladies these days.

"Okay, he's busy, so—?"

The girl lifted her shoulders briefly. "You'll have to just wait. I'll give him the room number."

"No," Clay tried again. It was like pushing a boulder through a swamp, summoning up enough energy to even try to get this girl to do something. A part of his mind stood back and viewed himself with wonder. He should be the kind of figure that inspired a little respect, a little jump-to-it from other people. He was a hitter, for God's sake, a killer in the employ of a very good execution company. Well, what used to be a very good execution company. Regency's quality had been slipping for awhile but its reputation had only started to slide very recently.

He shook his head. This was part of the problem. He couldn't even finish a thought these days without interrupting himself with some namby pamby, beside-the-point drivel. No wonder no one was intimidated. No wonder they all treated him like a ghost.

He cleared his throat. "Look it's *very* cold, and getting colder. Call Luis, great, but in the meantime, you need to get me another room."

"Oh, we don't have any."

A flicker of anger in his gut. Clay tried to keep it in view, wanting to coax the flame higher. He pulled the blinds up, rubbed frost from his motel room window and pushed the comm up to the glass so the girl could enjoy the view of the parking lot. There were a couple of trucks parked down at the far end and exactly four cars pulled up in front of rooms.

"How many people've you got staying here right now?" he asked. "Versus how many rooms in this dump?" Dump. Sheesh, there was a weak word. Why was he asking questions anyway? Why wasn't he telling this idiot girl exactly what she was going to do? Why—

Yeah . . . more questions. He couldn't seem to stop with the questions.

"That's because we can't rent out all the rooms," the girl said. "They got to have stuff fixed first. Some of them are, you know. Pretty bad."

Clay looked around the pit that was his own room and imagined how much worse 'pretty bad' could be.

"Listen," he said, hearing the monotone of his voice. He tried—and failed—to shove some conviction into his words. "I'm going out for some dinner. I'll be back in an hour. If the heat's not working, I'm leaving. And you're not charging a dime for anything, including last night."

The gum snapped. "But Marty always says I'm not authorized to—"

Clay shut the connection. Weak. God, he was weak. The girl was probably thinking the same thing Garity had when Clay opened the door to him: soft, lumpy, old slob.

The temperature had dropped noticeably while they were talking. His skin was gooseflesh. Rummaging in the suitcase open at the foot of the bed, he pulled out a heavy gray sweatshirt, yanked it over his head, and considered where he might go to kill some time while waiting for Luis to show up and do his thing.

He thought about Garity, how the other hitter had already done his recon, familiarized himself with the lay of the land around the penitentiary. The most elementary, most basic and vital part of prepping for a job, but somehow Clay had passed the better part of two days between this room, a couple of fast food joints, and the liquor store, and never once had it crossed his mind to head toward the job site.

He supposed he could get it over with now. Too bad the weather had gone to shit.

He crouched beside the bed, fumbling under it for the thick hiking boots he'd brought to wear during the capture-and-kill procedure on the poor sap being released from the penitentiary in the morning. The boots were jammed up against a couple of cases he'd stowed beneath the bed upon arrival and never touched since.

In the first case nestled the Caiman 240, tomorrow's initial weapon of choice. This was the rifle he would use to wound the Executable just enough so that the man would have to stop running. Assuming Garity didn't lame the E first, which Garity almost certainly would.

The other job-related items he'd brought were in the second case. These were items necessary to fulfill the details of this particular contract: wire, half a roll of duct tape, bottle of hydrochloric acid, bleach, box cutter, rubber tubing, pliers. This job was going to be a major pain in the ass.

He'd always been a one-and-done, just-shoot-the-poor-bastard-already kind of hitter. And yeah, maybe that was partly because those jobs were so much quicker and easier, but—just as a matter of personal preference—he'd never been into hits that involved torture before the final blow. He could do those kinds of jobs, had done his share of them over the years, in fact. Nobody had ever seen him flinch or heard him complain. He just didn't *prefer* them, that was all and usually numbed himself up before and after. He used to employ a kind of self-taught meditation before the really unpleasant jobs, concentrated on a blank gray wall in his mind until he made himself equally blank, with flat thoughts and zero engagement with the world around him. More recently, he'd used a few drinks to achieve a similar effect.

Merle Edgers didn't know about the drinking but he knew about Clay's preferences and, when assigning jobs, had always tried to respect those whenever possible. And why not? Regency had a few killers on staff who clamored to fulfill those particular contracts.

But Edgers wasn't respecting Clay's preferences this time, was he? Because there was no other hitter available to take the job? Or had he found out that Clay was drinking maybe a little too much, getting a little sloppy? This might be Edgers' way to get Clay to quit, to retire permanently to that silent apartment with a whiskey bottle for a wife.

Okay. Clay creaked up from his knees. Time to stop thinking and start doing. Get the recon done before dark, eat a solid meal at some restaurant or other, didn't matter which, then see what Luis had wrought back here in room 124.

The pistol he habitually carried was on the dresser between his comm and a motel-provided stack of faded brochures for pirate miniature golf courses and down-home barbecue restaurants. He slipped it under his belt before tugging on his down parka, hat and gloves. As he turned toward the door, he glimpsed himself in the full-length mirror on the wall. He looked like a giant stuffed mushroom, plump, soft and colorless.

As soon as he stepped outside, wind rattled the nylon of his parka. Jesus, it felt like it was already colder than ten degrees. They must be heading below zero tonight. The world was made entirely of pewter: the concrete lot, the sky, the motel's metal siding, the sleet slicing up the air like tiny bits of blade.

He hurried toward his car and almost went down on his butt. His arms pinwheeled, his parka-encased torso lurching this way and that as he struggled to regain his balance.

Ice had collected on the windshield of his car in tiny white pellets as if someone had gutted a bean bag animal just above the glass. The wiper blades were half-buried in the stuff. And beneath the pellets, a smooth glaze of ice coated the entire outside of the car. He tugged at the door handle. The door resisted. He pulled harder. Nothing budged.

"Oh, c'mon," he muttered, shuffling back to try the rear door. This one gradually unstuck itself, but required him to use not only all his arm strength, but to lean back so as to add his full body weight to the effort. When the door finally swung free, the suddenness set him scrambling off-balance again.

He climbed into the back, pulled the door shut behind him, then crawled over the console between the two front seats. His knee flared up again. When he'd managed to reassemble himself upright in the driver's seat, he blasted the defroster and stretched his legs out as straight as he could. His left knee wasn't too bad, but the right felt like it had a nest of pissed-off scorpions lodged just under the kneecap.

The ice on the windshield gradually melted. He gave it five minutes, watching sleet dissolve on the glass, then another five. By that point, the pain had subsided in intensity, but not disappeared. Darkness was coming on fast. He didn't relish checking out the prison exit or the woods surrounding the prison's perimeter where he and Garity would have to position themselves for that first shot in the morning. But it was only going to get darker, colder, and icier so he should really get a move on.

Putting the car into drive, he jolted across the ruts in the parking lot. There were too many to avoid them entirely. Bad for the suspension, but that was just another 'thing to deal with' down the road. The lot was sufficiently rough with gravel and potholes that at least the tires kept decent traction.

The main road was a different story. He turned too carelessly onto it. The rear of the car fishtailed across the oncoming lane, swinging back over the center line about two seconds before a pickup truck would have smashed into it. The truck's horn blasted as it passed by, the sound carrying back toward Clay on the wind.

He examined his hands on the steering wheel. Steady. He narrowed his eyes, feeling the rhythm of his heart in his chest. Unchanged. Where was the adrenaline? The startle reflex? Then he looked down at the speedometer and registered that he still hadn't slowed down.

Why slow down? The stretch of two-lane through town was flat and he was at the outskirts of it already. Traffic was practically nonexistent. Night was smothering down over them all and he just wanted to get the damn prep work done so he could settle into a diner or a burger joint with a hot coffee and then find some kind of room, somewhere, and fold himself onto the bed and maybe never wake up.

Or maybe he needed that coffee now, to gird himself for the recon. Wasn't there a little coffee hutch down one of these side streets? Maybe this one, King Street. He made the turn and sped down the block. No, this didn't look ri—

The loss of traction was sudden and shocking. He threw the steering wheel into the direction of the slide. *There's your adrenaline!* some jokey voice at the back of his brain shouted. *About time!* The brake pedal fluttered under his foot, but there was no stopping a 2,000-pound bulk of metal gliding sideways with 35 miles per hour of momentum pushing it along. The tires smashed up over a high curb. A rending of metal against metal tore through the scratch of sleet against glass. The car juddered violently, then was still.

A curtain airbag enveloped the left side of Clay's head. He let the weight of his skull sink into it for a moment. It was cool and smelled faintly chemical. Like medicine. The car was silent except for the sound of the sleet. The interior felt pleasantly insulated. He pulled himself upright, blinked at the rearview mirror.

Green and white filled the reflection, green lettering that was stocky and no-nonsense despite having been twisted aslant by the impact of car against signpost. The letters were backwards in the mirror, but he had no trouble reading them.

Parking Reserved
Guardian Angels Parish Visitors Only

He raised an arm to push at the airbag. A dull ache radiated from the ribs on his left side. At the same moment he noticed a stronger ache rising from his neck and across the back of his skull, spreading like fungus toward the crown of his head and he pressed a hand to the nape of his neck. He seemed to be intact, but any recon was surely down the tubes for the night.

Relief rinsed through him. Not prepping was *the* cardinal sin in the execution business, but—well, prepping was another thing he'd deal with tomorrow.

Something tapped against the driver's side window, whatever it was obscured by the side airbag. It kept tapping, at the same anxious pace.

Wincing at the pain in his ribs, Clay shoved the airbag aside.

A man on the other side of the glass peered into the car, the knuckle of his bent index finger upraised and still poised in midair. The man's hand was bare, the fingers bony. The skin stretched across the knucklebone was dry and cracked with what looked like dried blood edging the crevices where the skin had split.

Clay's first thought was: Charlie Manson. The man outside the car had the same scrawny, chicken-bone build, the flyaway Jesus-with-bedhead hair, the skimpy goatee.

But, at second glance, this man lacked the maniacal glare to the eyes. He looked concerned, but not at all panicked.

Clay was about to lower the window, but then he thought *what the hell* and pushed at the door. It didn't open right away and he remembered that it had been frozen shut. He put his shoulder into it—his ribs protested but only a little—and the door swung wide. The scrawny man had to backpedal to avoid getting smashed by it.

"You okay?" the man asked. His voice was as scrawny and light as the rest of him.

Well, I've avoided the synth caps so far today, that jokey voice wheezed in Clay's head again. *Does that count as okay?*

"I think . . . I guess so," Clay said and went around to the back of the car to check the damage. Part of the rear bumper dangled toward the sleet-crusted grass. The trunk was crushed in, holding the parking sign's metal pole in a close embrace. The tires on that side looked basically okay so he should be able to drive away if he didn't mind leaving a tottering signpost in his wake, which he didn't.

And go do the recon after all? He physically sagged at the thought, leaning his weight against an intact portion of trunk.

"Hey." The scrawny guy moved in closer. "You don't want to fool around with car wrecks."

"Just a little fender bender." But Clay remained slumped against the car, his head bent so he saw nothing but the dark blue metal and the sleet bouncing off it.

"Hey, even a fender bender, you can mess up your neck, screw up your back. Hey, you should at least come inside, get warm. Father Ray can call about the sign if you want. Except it's Saturday."

Clay raised his head. "Call who?"

"Well, whoever needs calling. Street department? Don't they do the signs? Bet they'll want you to pay the full freight to replace it though. The city budget's in the toilet. The police might—"

"No." Clay pronounced the word with absolute finality.

"No police?"

"No police."

The scrawny guy hadn't seemed to notice the stain of beer fumes on Clay's breath, but the police sure would. Not that he was drunk by any stretch, or even impaired. He just wasn't sure he could count on a breathalyzer to confirm that fact. Also, now that he considered the matter, he couldn't be entirely certain that he didn't have a couple of green-and-yellow-striped pills in the glove box. Little Quakes, younger cousin to synth, with much milder highs and nothing like synth's piranha reputation. But still illegal.

If Regency wanted to can him, what better excuse than a DUI or worse, drug bust, while on a job? Even if Clay felt no excitement about the next day's job, he wouldn't say no to the money. Child support bloodied up the bank account the first of every month, like clockwork.

The man hadn't drawn back. In fact, he'd actually moved closer. He met Clay's gaze. The man's eyes were a shade of gray that was strangely warm and soft. The color reminded Clay of some kind of bird—a dove or a pigeon, maybe—feathers shifting gently with each breath.

"Hey, whatever it is," the man said quietly, "stolen car, drugs, outstanding warrants—hell, everything short of jailbreak, I have been there, sir. I have been there. So I don't judge people, you know what I mean?"

Clay opened his mouth, about to offer some kind of explanation, some defense of himself, but what should have been a matter of a few words—I'm not a car thief, I'm not a synthfreak, I'm just your basic, boring taxpayer, with a full-time job and unexpired tags—swelled into something that he had no idea how to say.

"You look like you could use a hot meal." The man briefly touched Clay's shoulder. Clay twitched away from the contact. "My name's Jimmy. I was about to go in, get something to eat."

Clay looked around. This entire block looked to be church property, a good-sized chunk of real estate populated by the church itself and several smaller buildings of similar architecture.

"Where?"

"In there. Social hall in the basement." Jimmy swept one thin hand at the church behind them before curling the fingers against the cold and jamming his fist into his jacket pocket. "They've got a big kitchen too. Those industrial-sized mixers and sinks, you know? What's your name?"

"Mike." It was Clay's standard, automatic answer when anyone who didn't need to know his real name asked that question.

He tilted his head back. The church's gray stones bulked together, massing upward to a red-tiled roof from which a number of tiles were missing. Cracks ran in crazed lines between the stones. The yellowed bones of weeds hung over the edges of the gutters high overhead. Even so, the building had a dignity of age and size that no amount of disrepair could destroy.

We will outlast you the stones seemed to whisper.

No shit, Clay thought in reply.

Jimmy turned back by the iron gate that led into the churchyard. "You coming?" he called to Clay who stood where Jimmy had left him. Jimmy, misunderstanding, added, "We can deal with the car later. Even if you— uh—borrowed it. The cops are going to have a load of wrecks to deal with tonight."

Clay pawed one thickly-gloved hand across his cheek. The world was a fog of ice and low cloud and so was his brain. He couldn't think, couldn't make a decision, couldn't take a step.

Jimmy patted one of the frosted spikes ornamenting the top of the gate. "Just have some coffee. Get warm."

Nodding too many times, Clay managed to shift his legs into gear and shuffle to the gate where Jimmy waited for him. The sidewalk was treacherous here, ice covering old bricks the exact color of any number of dried bloodstains that Clay had seen over the years.

Inside the gate, irregular flagstones led to a narrow stairway that descended to a windowless metal door. The door surprised Clay, and unsettled him. It was ugly and featureless, industrial, like a door on a loading dock. Like a job demanding to be done, and the blank metal of the gun required to do it.

Both men gripped the icy railing as they crept down step by step. Jimmy pushed the door. It wheezed open in a burst of yellow and white light, smells of chicken and cornbread, voices stacked upon voices.

Clay stopped dead in the doorway. Sleet nailed his back; heat smothered his front. Jimmy came back to grasp his elbow and start him moving forward again.

From now on, Clay thought, whenever he heard the phrase 'social hall' (not that those were words he heard often), he'd know that was church code for 'old basement'.

"Serving line's over this way." Jimmy tugged him that direction. "There's a couple old ladies here cook a pretty mean fried chicken when we get enough meat donated."

The basement was packed with men, women, and kids filling cafeteria tables that ran the length of the room. Infants squirmed under frayed blankets in carriers. Toddlers waddled up and down the aisles. Everyone was talking at once. So many people. Too many. Clay was used to empty places, the aloneness of his apartment and motel rooms.

He averted his eyes from the people, letting his gaze jump around the room. The walls were brick painted a thick and lumpy beige. The ceiling was low and glaringly white. He had the impression of a heavy cloth about to come down over them all. Scuff marks and snow melt soiled the linoleum floor. The heat was unbearable. No wonder the babies were squalling like a pack of demons.

"End of the line," Jimmy said. Clay stared at him. "Food line," Jimmy added.

They each took a tray and set it on the silver runners. Clay realized he was starving. He slid his tray along the tracks, pausing at each basin of food to let a worker tong a chicken thigh onto his plate or scoop a mound of mashed potatoes beside the meat. Cornbread, green beans, pecan pie—and most of it looked homemade. How long had it been since he'd had homemade fried chicken? Had he *ever* had homemade fried chicken? He'd been a late baby, grandparents all dead before he knew them and anyway, in the few vids that remained, they'd appeared to be more intent on slinging back some drinks than on dragging a deep fryer out of the cupboard.

He picked up his tray and surveyed the tables, noting how haphazard the various diners looked. Patchy coats and droopy, stretched-out sweaters, scratchy beards, uneven haircuts or, in the case of a few kids, what had to be genuine bowl cuts. Some of the women reminded him of greyhounds, worry and poverty thinning their features to bone.

"Hey, there's some room," Jimmy said, jerking his head at a table at the far end.

Clay turned to him. "Is this a soup kitchen?"

Jimmy laughed. "Is this the 1930's?" He nudged Clay with one elbow. "Hey, I'm joking. I've never heard anybody call it that, but, yeah. Basically. They've got free dinner here five nights a week. There's a lot of need in this town. In the whole county."

Clay eyed a grimy, unshaven man, probably not too far off his own age, passing by on his way for seconds. "Listen," Clay said. "I've got a job. I'm not some homeless guy. I don't need to be here."

Jimmy raised both eyebrows. They were thin squiggles above his squinting eyes. "You so sure about that? You don't have to be embarrassed. Nobody here's doing real great, not money-wise."

He headed for the empty table. Clay, staring after him, gripped his tray with one hand and raised the other, running his fingertips across his stubbly cheek. The stubble was long enough that it was starting to curl at the ends. At what point did you have to admit you'd neglected shaving long enough for the stubble to turn into outright whiskers?

When had he last showered anyway? Not in the motel, not that last night at home, maybe not even the night before that. It all jumbled in his head now, fragments of memory sloshing around his skull in a brain-stew. No wonder Garity had been so reluctant to come into the motel room. Clay probably stank. But that wasn't the same thing as living in a cardboard box.

He re-gripped the tray with both hands and followed Jimmy.

They both ate quickly and voraciously as soon as they sat down. What appeared to be an enormous extended family, from withered great grandparents down to yet another squalling infant, occupied the rest of the table. The family talked and talked, the noise overwhelming the small pool of quiet at the end where Clay and Jimmy sat.

A man in black shirt and pants and a white clerical collar came over, tray in hand but with a modest amount of food on the plate, and slid in between what looked like two octogenarians. They both grinned at him, their chins dripping chicken grease, and immediately set to chatting.

"That's Father Ray," Jimmy said, noticing that Clay was watching. "Parish priest. The regular congregation's gotten pretty small, but he keeps things going somehow. He's a good guy. You can tell him anything."

"Anything?" Clay asked, skeptical.

Jimmy sopped up grease with his cornbread. "I trust him more than anybody I know. He doesn't talk no matter what bad stuff you fess up to."

Fess up? Tell some stranger everything you'd done, every miserable thought that crawled through your head? Weird and surely distasteful, but then what religion wasn't totally nuts?

"You don't do that whole confession bit," Clay said.

Jimmy shook his head. "I'm not Catholic. I just talk to the guy. It helps with some of the worst stuff." He tapped his head just above one ear. "In here, you know?"

Clay was shaking his head right back at Jimmy. "Some guy you barely know?"

Jimmy laughed. "I've been hanging around this town for twenty years."

Hard to imagine anyone coming to this dismal little town from somewhere else. No, this was a place for native-born and only the hard-up cases at that.

Jimmy was still smiling, a lopsided twist to the mouth that looked odd and, because he seemed completely unaware of its oddness, entirely sincere. It was not the kind of smile Clay was used to. In his world, smiles came in three varieties: lying, cruel, and superior. Jimmy's head dipped for just a couple of seconds, like he was diving down to fetch something. Resolve, maybe, a decision. When he raised his head, he still had that smile, but his eyes were serious and they held tight to Clay's own gaze.

"I've been here ever since the day they let me out of the prison," Jimmy said.

Clay shouldn't have been surprised—this was a prison town, that's where a good chunk of the people with jobs worked and no reason an ex-inmate with nowhere to go might not stick around—and yet he was. Maybe it was Jimmy's mildness, the clarity of his expression. He didn't act like a man with anything to hide.

And, well, he wasn't hiding anything, was he, but announcing it to a stranger instead?

Clay took another forkful of pecan pie. It was drizzled with chocolate and, at that moment, seemed like quite possibly the best piece of pie he'd ever eaten. It had been a long time since he'd really tasted anything he ate. Meals were a matter of transporting a sufficient number of calories into his mouth and chewing well enough for his system to process them. He let his tongue push the creaminess back and forth against the roof of his mouth.

He swallowed, brought up another forkful and asked, "Car theft? You seem to have a certain fixation on that. Or maybe that's because of what just happened to me?"

Jimmy wasn't smiling now, but he didn't flinch or turn away. "Car theft was just the beginning. I was in for ten years. Murder two."

Clay lowered the fork. "You're shitting me."

"Why would I do that?"

No particular reason came to mind. "Because that's what cons—and ex-cons—do. They con people. Just for the hell of it if nothing else."

"You really think I'm making this up?" Jimmy sat where he was, motionless, his tray pushed to one side and his hands folded calmly on the table in front of him.

Those feather-gray eyes were clear and true. Not the eyes of a liar or a scammer although Clay had seen too many eyes—like too many smiles—that employed ruthless and convincing deceit. He rubbed the back of his neck. The headache had retrenched, was digging in its claws again. What was he doing here? The heat was probably working in his room by now, or he'd find another room, maybe where Garity was staying. The car was drivable. He just needed to get in it and head to—

"I'm not just a felon," Jimmy said as if there had been no long pause in the conversation. "I'm an Executable."

A peculiar heat crawled through Clay's body. His mouth was dry. He fumbled for the glass of water on his tray.

Jimmy just sat there, leaning comfortably forward, his forearms resting on the tabletop. Only the tight hunch of his shoulders and the lines that cut deeper around his eyes revealed that he wasn't as relaxed as he first appeared.

"Now I know you're putting me on," Clay said even though he knew no such thing and strongly suspected that Jimmy was telling the bare truth. "Executables don't go around telling strangers—telling anyone—that they're Executables. Doesn't happen."

"Doesn't usually happen."

Clay was shaking his head. "Does *not* happen. You'd have way too much to lose. Like, everything."

"Maybe I decided to take a chance." As Jimmy spoke, his shoulders relaxed and the lines of his face softened. "I've been here for a long time. Father Ray lets me live in the rectory, a spare room on the top floor."

"How do you make it? Executables can't work, not legally."

"I help with stuff at the church, handyman-type stuff. Keep a low profile, you know? He never asked any questions but I told him I was a bum who got tired of the road. I couldn't have got an apartment or a real job, not with that E branded on my ID."

Clay glanced down the table. The priest was listening intently to a little girl clutching a stuffed cat. "And he never asked about anything."

"No. He just treated me all right. But after I got to know him and some other people here at the church, I told them the truth."

This was ridiculous. Crazy. If this guy was a felon, he was the most innocent, naïve sample of the species that Clay had ever met. Executables huddled in the dark, emerging to sling drugs or earn a nice stash for the pimp who gave them a cot in a room crowded with his other whores. Executables did not break their silence and they did not live in the sunlight.

"And?"

"And it was okay."

A rare sensation of curiosity and of something else—hope? The possibility of reprieve?—quivered at the periphery of Clay's mind. "It was okay," Clay repeated, stepping lightly from word to word like he was balancing on stones set across deep water.

"I got tired of lying about what I was, I guess." Jimmy broke into a grin that, despite his crooked, yellow teeth, achieved brilliance through sheer—what? Happiness? Contentment?

How was that even possible, Clay thought. His mouth twitched involuntarily into a whisper of a smile.

"Maybe you should give it a try." Jimmy straightened, leaned comfortably back.

"What?"

"Hang out here for a couple of days."

"And do what?"

A shrug. "Just be with us. Give yourself a break or a chance or whatever it is you need." He shifted on the bench and leaned forward again, the grin gone, but a warmth lingering around the corners of his mouth. "Because—and don't be insulted, hey—it's pretty obvious you need something. And I don't think it was just coincidence, you running into that pole."

Clay stiffened. Here it came. The God talk. Same old thing. Just like Lucy before she took the kids and moved a hundred miles away. And what good was any of it if you didn't believe it? Here was this guy, an Executable of all things, and he looked so damn content, so pleased with his lot, "hanging out" with all the other God people. It wasn't fair. Maybe Clay wouldn't have minded having a little of that for himself, but a man couldn't just make himself believe.

Hope limped away and disappointment gimped in to fill the empty space. Despair lifted its sagging head and showed Clay a dead, blank face.

The man was an Executable! Why should he get to sleep peacefully all night when, God knows, Clay didn't? Why should he be sitting here, safe and sound, talking about his comfortable place at the rectory and all the friends he trusted and who were so loyal to him? Clay's own apartment was sour and stale and no one but himself ever set foot in it. Not even his kids since they never wanted to visit and he knew Lucy talked shit about him in front of them.

Heat crackled along his nerves, singeing each tendril. He welcomed his anger and sense of outrage and coaxed the flames higher. For the first time that day, he didn't want to die.

He soothed his throat with another gulp of water. "Riiiight. So you trust your people and you tell them the truth. But then these friends of yours tell other people—some not so big on the trust business—and next thing you know, you've got Elite or Eye for Eye or, or maybe Regency or one of those outfits right back on your tail again. And you're a dead man. Maybe a very slow and messy dead man." Clay frowned, his thoughts skipping to the specifications laid out for tomorrow's job. Talk about snail-slow and messy as all hell. Hell for the E and hell for the hitter stuck with the job. While this guy sat here, smug as you please, nothing more harrowing than shoveling snow on his horizon.

"It was a long time ago," Jimmy said. "I think they've all moved on."

Clay snorted. "Execution companies never move on. You know why?"

Jimmy shook his head.

"Because," Clay explained, "even if they track you down five years, ten years, twenty years after you get out, those bonuses in the original contract still hold true. That bonus money is held in a fund—like a—a—an escrow kind of thing, you know?"

Jimmy just stared at him. Maybe Clay was imagining it, but the man's eyes didn't seem quite as clear or feather-soft.

Clay continued. "You know, so the client's already paid the money into the fund at the bank at the time they signed the contract. An irrevocable deal, right? So there's still going to be a nice payout as soon as they bag you. And verify the remains, of course."

Wincing, Jimmy straightened and sat back.

"Sorry," Clay added. "There's not really a nice way to put it."

"You sound like you know a lot about this." Jimmy's voice was tentative and strained. Were those shadows gathering under his eyes, in the hollows of his skinny cheeks, turning him into a skull right in front of Clay?

Good.

"Not so much," Clay said.

"You have dealings up at the prison?"

"Not so much," Clay answered again and was pleased to see the little guy practically squirm. "Just a little. You know, tangentially."

Jimmy jumped up, grabbed his tray. "I'm gonna go get rid of this," he mumbled, his eyes flicking down to the other end of the table where Father Ray was laughing so hard with his dining companions that he slapped the table.

"Hey, Jimmy," Clay said and the other man stopped. "Why'd you tell me? You don't know me. So why?"

Jimmy was off-balance, silverware sliding down the slope of his tray. "I guess . . ." He hesitated. "I guess because you seemed so alone. Same as I was. And, hey, somebody gave me a chance, you know?"

Humiliation flamed along the same pathways where anger had burned. So Clay carried the stink of failure and isolation with him. People like Garity saw right through him. Even a lousy Executable felt sorry for him.

Well, it wouldn't take long to snuff out Jimmy's pity.

"Jimmy," he said again, voice casual. "What company was it had the contract exactly? Did you ever find out?"

Jimmy worked his jaw once sideways, then spun away with the tray, sliding among the other diners who'd finished eating and were crowding the trash cans and the tray return bin.

Clay pulled out his comm, glanced over to make sure that Jimmy had looked back and seen him with the device. Make the idiot—the trusting, happy idiot—worry. The weather forecast blizzarded the screen—more snow, more unbearable cold—and he considered briefly how, through Regency, he could look up any E if he chose to, find out all the particulars including which agency stood to benefit from a kill. He wouldn't get the bonus money, but the agency that did would owe him a return favor. Might give him a tip on a quarry's location someday.

And really, did it matter if the contract was with Regency or some other company? No question a contract existed or the other man wouldn't have gotten so squirrely so fast at a hint of his world sliding sideways.

Was Jimmy—James—even the man's real name? No E could ever get that comfortable, right? Complacency was not a healthy state of mind for an Executable.

Yeah, and apathy wasn't a healthy state of mind for a killer.

He didn't know how it was possible, but he could already feel his outrage seeping away and the old lethargy flowing in to take its place. The flat boredom, the excruciating monotony that stood ready to suffocate him every day. What the hell would it take to smash that flatness into a thousand pieces and finally be free of it?

Unfair! He tried to use the word like a whip to scourge himself to action. Unfair that an E had a better life than he did. That was flat wrong. An injustice. Unfair! *C'mon, Clay*, he flailed at himself. *Feel something, do something.* Be *something for a goddamn change. Whatever the hell you believe or don't believe, don't just sit here. Climb out of the nothingness that you are . . .*

He flung himself up from the bench, leaving his tray. His hand went to his waist where the gun waited. But he didn't pull it out. Not yet.

People were leaving now, floods of them, up the same steps that led to the churchyard. But the Executable had gone up a different set of stairs. Clay followed him.

These stairs were wider, higher, three turns to reach the top. They released him into a corridor lit only by exit signs and a dim illumination that flickered from shadowy alcoves cut into the walls at regular intervals. The ceiling was lost in darkness high overhead. The chipped marble floor emanated a coldness that was profound.

Clay paused at the top of the stairs. The voices rising up from the basement gradually thinned out, moved away. He listened to the silence spread out before him and pondered which alcove Jimmy was hiding in. Clay had come up the staircase too fast behind Jimmy for Jimmy to have made it farther than this.

His eyes closed for several seconds as he listened. From inside these thick walls, he couldn't hear sleet or the sound of car tires crushing snow on the street out front. What he could hear was a gusty howl of wind bursting periodically through some chimney or pipe or a chink between stones. That, and mild buzzing that seemed to come from multiple locations, each slightly out of sync with the others.

How many times had he done this exact same thing? Eyes closed, ears wide, alert for the sound of someone shifting position ever so slightly to relieve a cramped muscle or for the breath a terrified person was no longer able to keep in check.

And what the hell was he doing messing with this when he had more of the same shit already on his plate tomorrow and next week and next month?

And hadn't he already asked himself that question? How did a person shut down the questions before the questions drove him completely and totally batshit crazy?

Get motivated, he commanded himself, and set his body in motion. *Come on, Clay*, he pleaded with himself, *don't be so goddamn pathetic*. He meant to glide along the corridor, but could only be bothered to lumber. At each alcove, he paused.

Each held a statue of a saint on a pedestal with a pair of electric candles buzzing gently at the saint's feet. Pots of fake greenery were set about to form a dense shrubbery, the leaves dull with dust in the dim light. The saints appeared uniformly mild-faced and smooth-skinned although closer inspection revealed decay evident in chipped paint and occasional fingers broken off at the knuckle. Some held peculiar objects—a spoked wheel, a harp, a pair of eyeballs on a plate—and they all seemed to be staring at something slightly above Clay's head.

There it was. A shifting sound, soft as a sigh, punctuated by a faint crack. An arthritic knee joint popping, most likely. Clay could relate to that.

He headed toward the next alcove on the left. It was silent again except for the buzzing of the candles. The saint stared at Clay rather than above him, but only because the statue's eyes happened to be on a level with Clay's. Whoever this saint was, he must have died by decapitation and now clutched his own stony head in front of his chest.

Leaves to the statue's left rippled slightly. Now Clay heard the breathing. Light, fast, and desperate. He freed his gun, considered the lack of a silencer, decided it didn't matter. An Executable was fair game.

He snubbed the gun forward and used his foot to shove one of the planters aside, revealing a shoe, part of a leg, a protruding elbow. Crinkling sounds as the E tried to compress himself behind the foliage that remained.

Clay pushed at another planter with his foot, tilting it. It toppled onto the marble. The ceramic shattered, the crash echoing down the corridor.

Completely exposed, the E huddled behind the decapitated saint. He looked up, blinking at Clay. Those eyes—Jesus, they looked wounded deep inside, like Clay was some kind of long-time friend caught in the act of betrayal.

At least you've got a place, Clay thought, staring at the man, trying to work up the anger and humiliation he'd felt earlier. *You've had your happiness. And you're just an E. A lousy, goddamn E.*

It was like trying to work up saliva in a too-dry mouth. Feeling no humiliation, no anger, feeling absolutely nothing at all but hoping he still might, Clay pulled the trigger.

The sound of the gunshot echoed off the stone walls and rang against the ceiling. Then there was nothing but the eternal buzz of the plastic flame and the blood that spattered the saint's robes and pooled below his feet.

"Goddamn," Clay muttered.

Nothing had changed. In these seconds after the killing, he felt precisely the same as in the seconds before the killing.

No, not precisely the same. The emptiness that always hollowed him out these days had something in it now. Something that tasted like salt water and grief. A flight missed, a message inadvertently deleted, a phone call never returned.

From somewhere at the bottom of the stairs, he heard a shout and footsteps. At first, he couldn't move. Stood frozen in the grip of some thought he couldn't quite catch. An emotion he couldn't exactly identify.

The shouts grew louder. He shook himself. Had to clear out the oddness from his brain. None of it meant anything. He was just getting old. Burned out. But goddamn, he would still force himself to function.

From somewhere at the bottom of the stairs, he heard a shout and footsteps.

He moved away, toward the big church doors at the far end of the corridor. He was a licensed hitter taking out a registered E felon. No crime, but he didn't think he could endure the boring and pointless rituals that always ensued immediately after the hit. Maybe tomorrow.

He pushed aside the heavy door and slipped outside. The cold was intense, snow blowing in great, blinding gusts that stung his face and numbed his skin. Wind bit instantly through his layers of clothing. He hurried to the car, started the engine, blasted the heat, and eased carefully away from the wreckage of the signpost. Halfway down the next block, he glanced in the mirror. That great bulk of stone was already lost behind him, drowned by whirling clouds of snow.

He paused at the intersection. His comm was pinging. He pulled it out, checked the call, flicked it to audio only.

The girl from the Crescent Moon office sounded like she was chewing the same wad of gum. She snapped it noisily. "Luis said to tell you he got the heat fixed so you can come back whenever." She closed the connection.

"Great," Clay whispered to the black screen. His voice was hoarse. "Isn't that great news."

The same room, the same dead air, soccer games that might as well be the same teams playing the same matches. Another night on gritty sheets, trying to lose consciousness for a few hours. And then out into the blackness of early morning, frostbite-cold, and a job he didn't want to deal with.

He drove along the main road, back toward the motel. He drove carefully now, not because his earlier accident scared him, but because a wreck would mean a delay and he needed to get back to the room and the synth caps. He didn't know why he'd bothered to kill Jimmy. He'd killed enough people. He should have known that couldn't give him anything, couldn't pull him out of this swamp.

But the synth? It was time for them now. He imagined how their red carapaces would gleam when he opened the pill case and the light struck them.

Red as blood, red as anger, red as life.

His last hope.

RAYFID & BIDDY

FOR A FEW SWEET SECONDS, Rafe thought he'd
lost them.

The building he backed against was damp from the
rain, the bricks still warm from the ninety-five degree
heat earlier that day. Rafe's chest heaved with each
breath. His lungs were on fire and sweat smeared his
vision. The rabbit in him knew that if they guessed
which alley he'd jetted into, he was done. Baked.
Sayonara.

And then, shit, there they were. Both of them built
like refrigerators. Blocks of men. Rafe was wiry and
lean, a natural sprinter. No way they should have been
able to keep up with him. Too many chemicals in his
blood for too many years. Why hadn't he just slung the
product to the customers and kept it out of his own
veins? He was 24 years old and he was about to die.
Goddamn.

The white guy took the lead, smiling and squinting,
chin to his chest. His eyes bored down into Rafe's. A

hand the size of a paddle snagged Rafe by the shoulder, and another grabbed his hair.

"Why you runnin'? Huh?" the guy snarled, taking Rafe's head and twisting it into his armpit. The man reeked of cheap soap and sweat. "Why'd you make me chase you like that, you little bastard?"

Before Rafe could answer, the man's knuckles smashed him just under the sternum. All the air gusted out of Rafe's lungs. He hit the concrete with both knees and retched. Nothing came up, but his body heaved again.

"Not on the silks!" the white guy huffed. "You got to puke, you keep it on the leather!" Rafe spit and drooled next to the man's shoes. "Atta boy!" The man yanked Rafe back onto his feet. He cocked his fist for another punch, but before he could let it fly, his cohort stepped between them.

Rafe's benefactor was darker skinned, maybe East Asian or South American. He had almond-shaped eyes and irises as black as the pupils. "That's enough," he growled. "Biddy said he don't want him hurt. You bust him up, you tell Biddy why."

The white guy made a show of straightening his shoulders as he relinquished his grip on Rafe. "He takes off again and we got nothing to bring home, that's what you better be afraid of," he said.

A moment later, both men were behind Rafe. Someone gave him a powerful shove. He barely managed to keep his feet. One of the men—he didn't know which—let out an exasperated harumph. Rafe spat out some more phlegm. No blood, thank Jesus. He kept his eyes open for an exit, but nothing presented itself. The two men hung close; their foul garlic breath crowded him.

Just don't get caught, goddamn it, Owen had told him the previous night, as they practically bounced off the walls from meth and caffeine. Prepping for The Job. You get pinched, you get in a corner, you figure some way out of it, Owen said. This score is golden. We can't screw it up. Owen had been talking about the cops—tasers and batons, restraint ties and chokeholds—and the professional killers who worked for the execution companies. Biddy and the old crew had been the last thing on their minds.

Why did Rafe always have to be the fuckup? Why couldn't it be Owen shuffling along now with Biddy's thugs at his back? This was Rafe's score, damnit! Rafe had worked so hard on this one, so much legwork.

Owen? Shit. Owen just had the good luck that his girlfriend was the inside source they had to rely on for tips about the Executable's location. And without that particular information, all their plans were crap. If they couldn't find the Executable, they couldn't grab her, and if they couldn't grab her, they couldn't ransom her to the execution company. Which one was it? Oh, yeah. Regency. With an Inc after. Big time money.

So what had Rafe done to get on Biddy's shit list? Suspicion twisted in his gut. Had Owen done something, said something to make sure that Biddy would be all over Rafe right now, this particular night? Leaving Owen free to do the grab on his own and pocket the full ransom from Regency?

The two behemoths herded Rafe from the dilapidated Section 8 apartment houses toward the rubble of asphalt that passed for a street. A dark metallic sedan slipped into view, humming to an easy stop on the wrong side of the road. Dark-tinted glass retreated. The driver gripped the wheel with his right hand, while keeping his left arm slung along the door. He wore tight leather gloves that could serve him either in chauffeuring or smashing someone's sinus cavity; always ready for either. He poked his head slightly forward, diamonds glinting between his lips. Thelan—cool as always, and untouchable—was laughing at him.

"Rafe!" Thelan popped the door open and eased his long legs out. "Oh my God, where the hell have you been keeping yourself, boy?" He stood and indicated the rear door, then reached across and slid his fingers into the handle.

Rafe found himself seconds later sandwiched between his two escorts on the back seat. Thelan got behind the wheel again. His jacketed arm stretched along the back of the seat and his hand tapped the headrest. Rafe almost gagged on the thick scent of corn chips and bad cologne. "I didn't think you all could get this far on foot. Had to take the expressway and two exits." Thelan sounded half-impressed, half-mournful.

"Yeah, well," the white guy said, grabbing Rafe's stringy right bicep and giving it a shake. "He's been working out."

Thelan snickered. "Rafe is a special guest, Louis. I'm glad to see you didn't do anything unfortunate." Thelan glanced back, his smile unveiling the full set of gemstones in his front teeth. "This man and Biddy go way back, don't you, Rafe?"

Rafe wasn't sure how long he'd been doing part-time jobs for Biddy. They mostly consisted of slinging Peel caps to the low-end junkies and South Philly freakers, though Biddy put him wherever he needed him. Old City. Northeast. Olney. Kensington. When they'd first made acquaintance, Biddy was a hard-charging bull in the Peel business, with some side dealing into crystal and even heroin for the artistas and models he wooed. He had money and he had muscle, the two things Rafe lacked. Most of all, he had balls. Which, okay, Rafe had to admit, maybe he himself didn't have in abundance either.

And class. Damn. Biddy dressed in Armani Black Label, swilled Gran Patron and chomped down on Cuban Cohibas. The hard cash and benefits had kept Rafe at Biddy's beck and call for a long time. Too long. He'd seen more hardcore carnage than he'd ever cared to, and as time passed, it struck him that life expectancy in Biddy's organization was short and getting shorter all the time. People Rafe had shared some close confidence with kept disappearing.

So he'd decided to make himself a ghost, before someone else did it. Make his own scores—of which this one about to go down with Owen was by far the biggest—and when he had enough money, ditch out of Philly for good. He was going to start some place fresh, maybe Virginia Beach. Charlotte. Set up his own crew, stake his own claim. Buy his own cognac and his own cigarillos and be at the top of the food chain for a change. Be the shark in the smaller pond. To be his own master, that's all he wanted.

"You lucky Biddy sent the Sweet and Sour Lous here," Thelan said, eyeing Rafe in the rearview mirror. "And not one of the newer cadres. Some of those boys will fuck up your shit seriously."

The Lous. Well, it was easy to tell which was the Sour one. He'd released Rafe's bicep, but every couple of blocks gave him a jab in the ribs with his elbow. Sweet kept quiet, staring out the window and pinching his upper lip with his fingers. He didn't smell as bad, so Rafe leaned his way as the car lurched along.

Maybe there was still a chance to wrap up whatever this business was and still catch up with Owen for the score. But as soon as Thelan made a couple of corners, Rafe realized they weren't going where he'd expected. "We're not—" he croaked, trying to clear his throat and force down his sudden rising panic. "Not going downtown?"

"Ah nah, my brudda," Thelan said, effecting some phony Jamaican patois, giving a quick look back before turning on the radio and treating them to some old-school R&B on the sound system. "Biddy say he want to see you at The Clubhouse tonight."

The Clubhouse. Fuck me—

"That's right, Rafe," Sour Lou breathed into his ear, so close his incisors touched the flesh. "You're on my dance card, you little bitch."

Rafe's insides turned to water.

The ride felt endless. At every intersection, he clenched his hands and clenched his face and prayed they'd turn a different direction, away from the Clubhouse. Thirty-five minutes later, they pulled onto a darkened road where the only lights came from a single four-story brownstone with a couple of sports cars parked out front. All the other real estate on the east side was tallgrass, scrub brush and sickly-looking saplings that had sprung up on earth bulldozed years ago. There was an embankment about the length of a football field behind the building that sported some railroad track, and the tracts further along were zoned for foul-smelling industrial establishments.

The Clubhouse had originally belonged to a notorious East Coast biker gang, but they were no match for Biddy once he decided he wanted the property. The baddest asses in the biker herd got culled. And soon it was deemed more beneficial for the group to find a different place to gather. In a different city. In a different state. And Biddy got the deed to the Clubhouse.

Thelan parked on the wrong side of the street again, blocking in some Italian import with custom rims.

"C'mon, now," he said over his shoulder, climbing out.

Just the sight of that dour brownstone looming up at the edge of the street took the saliva right out of Rafe's mouth. He had a lot of memories of this place, none of them comfortable, and most of them very bad indeed. His legs didn't seem to want to move. He hunched in the car until the Lous prodded him out onto the remains of the sidewalk.

Thelan led them to the front doors of the Clubhouse, big oaken creations with heavy hinges and multiple bolt locks. They looked impenetrable. Maybe a team of howling Norsemen could cave them in with a medieval battering ram, but not those little play-toys the narco crews used to gain entry on the shotgun shacks in Methville. Thelan said a few low words to an ugly-looking cretin who was acting as a doorman, then into an intercom, then rocked back on his heels to wait.

Rafe's muscles tensed, ready for flight. His gaze skidded in every direction, searching for a way out.

Too late.

A couple of shadowy types opened the door and stepped aside to give them access to a foyer and, straight ahead, the elevator to the upper offices. Biddy had installed it while renovating the building.

As they waited for the elevator, Rafe snuck a peek down the staircase beside it. It had an ugly metal hand rail that angled into the shadows and disappeared. The Clubhouse basement. He shivered, though he wasn't cold. Below that was a sub-basement. Below that was the sub-sub, a dirt floor with a pit—

At first, he wasn't sure about the noise. Everything was surreal for him at this point, trying to stand upright amidst three guys that he knew wouldn't mind putting him through a gauntlet of swinging tire irons and two-by-fours. But then he heard it again, coming up from that shadowy netherworld, and his heart raced faster as he fought to stave off a horrifying memory—

A long, single, lonely howl.

Dogs. Goddamn feral dog pack. Holy fucking shit.

How could he get out of this? There were at least eight guys between him and the front door now. He had a quick fantasy of bowling them all over like pins, but that was quickly replaced by the much more likely vision of himself getting knocked to the floor and kicked into unconsciousness. Only to wake up to real horror.

Another piercing shriek and guttural moan from below. What was it with Biddy and goddamn dogs? He had his men take the truck out and round up the strays. Didn't feed them for a while, got them good and hungry, ready for any bloody piece of meat to dangle just above them—

The elevator door opened. A long mirror dominated its back wall. Rafe looked into his own eyes as he stepped inside. He looked terrified and beaten. The air was chilly in here. The same temperature as the rooms upstairs. Biddy didn't like to sweat in the offices. He didn't mind it when he was out and about, with his jacket off and doing some business with his own hands. But in the private offices, he liked it a constant 68 degrees. Said it kept the drinks chilled longer.

Rafe stared at the numbers above the door in agony. The elevator didn't move. Why wasn't it moving? Why the *hell* wasn't it moving? His chest tightened. He struggled to get enough air into his lungs. He needed the goddamn thing to move up. Up! Because if it moved down . . .

That meant they were going to the pit.

He felt like he was sucking air through a coffee stirrer at the memory of the place. Jesus, he hated it. Hated the cold, subterranean smell. Hated how, every time he'd had to go down there, he just about heaved up his lunch. Usually it was dog fights, Biddy's favorite sport. Rafe always grinned and shouted and slapped his betting money around, just like all the other guys, but underneath all that, he hated it.

When there was a person in the pit, it was even worse.

He didn't remember the particulars on the last guy, or why they'd had him hung out on some wire clad only in a blood-soaked cotton wifebeater. Just some tough who hadn't listened closely enough to Biddy. Rafe had his workman's gloves on, holding fast to his strand of piano wire, seeing but trying not to see. Every time there was a whistle, they'd ease up on the lines and lower the guy a little deeper into the pit. The dogs were going crazy, some of them leaping, snapping at toes. He'd been cut in the belly to get more dripping between his legs.

The gag had worked loose. Rafe could hear the man's screams above the insane growls and yelps of the animals below. No words. The man was way past words. The whistle again. Dropping him further, the wire ripping into his muscles and tendons, getting to the bone. Now two guys forcing his legs apart with more wires. The whistle again. Swinging him lower, the dogs making the first contact. Raucous laughter mixing in with the cacophony. Rafe had closed his eyes, bit on his tongue and pressed his lips against his teeth. Another fucking whistle—

Later, on the banks of the Schuylkill, they'd watched another bagged mess float off toward Delaware—

You done a good job for us tonight, Rafe.

Pause.

Nobody gone forget that.

No thank yous. No I am forever in your debt, you have my eternal gratitude, no I owe you one, I can never repay you, no we are friends forever, you and I, you'll always have a place in this organization—

The elevator shuddered. Rafe's legs threatened to collapse. Just fold right under him. But then—thank you, Jesus, sweet God Mary Jesus and Joseph—the elevator lurched upward. The numbers lit up, one by one, with a sweet Hallelujah ping.

Rafe gulped in lungfuls of cool air and steadied himself with one hand. It left a sweaty print on the mirror.

The elevator paused before the doors opened. Rafe forced himself to narrow his eyes. Tough guy. He had to keep it together. No need to tell Biddy about the score he and Owen had planned. Keep it all inside.

They stepped out onto luxurious burgundy carpet. The Lous crowded against him, pushing him down the hallway to Biddy's office. The door was already open, and the group parted to let Rafe enter first. In his mind, he put the mask on, the one to cover up everything. Zombie. Going zombie.

Biddy stood by the back wall of the room, where a good stretch of window had been sealed off and reinforced with steel. What view Biddy had was small, but that was no big deal. Biddy could look out on the city from many other vantage points, whether in this building or one of the many he controlled around town. He had cameras everywhere, eyes in the sky and crews to monitor it all. Hell, he had a gas grill on the rooftop of the Clubhouse.

A large screen on the adjacent wall broadcast a feed from the pit. Rafe's gaze skipped across it, back and forth. The lights glaring from the perimeter down into the hole were sharp and bright, crowding in, relentless as a migraine. The pit was empty, but only just. Some kind of fluid had recently drenched the dirt, churning it into filthy mud. The paw prints sunk all around in the muck were monstrous. Huge. The toenails had left gouges at least a couple of inches deep. Biddy'd got himself some new dogs. Beasts.

Rafe swallowed and shifted position, angling his entire body away from the screen. He needed to focus on Biddy right now, not on what had or hadn't happened down in the sub sub. Most especially, he didn't need to think about what might happen down there later that night.

He used to think he could guess Biddy's mood by what he was wearing, especially eyewear. If he had on clear lenses or his reading glasses, then everything would be all right. Holding up a tablet or a spreadsheet, looking over the rims expectantly as you walked into the room. That expression on his smooth caramel-colored features—good news? As the lenses got darker or more mirrored, the deeper was the hole you had to try to climb out of.

But eventually, Rafe had realized he was wrong. He didn't know the first thing about what was going on behind those crazy glittering brown-black eyes.

Rafe stopped just inside the doorway, and the Lous—who had anticipated this very event—took him by either arm and walked him toward a large polished ebony desk. In front of it was a single armless chair, his destination. Sweet Lou let his arm go, but Sour positioned him right in front of the chair and shoved him onto the cushioned seat with a thump.

"Sour! What the hell you think you're doing!" Biddy erupted, flinging a pair of large aviator sunglasses to the desktop with a clatter. In one long stride, he faced the goons with Rafe between them. Everybody in the room stiffened.

Sour Lou was a big man, but Biddy was a head taller and no slouch in the physique department. In a fair fistfight, they might have done equal damage to one another. In a cage match, once they hit the ground, Sour Lou might have even had a slight advantage, depending on position. In a fair fight. But not here. Not in Biddy's domain.

Sour gradually slumped and backed away. "Sorry—sorry," Lou offered, bending lower, smiling wide with his yellowed teeth. "I was—just trying to move it along."

Biddy raised an arm and indicated a place along the wall where Sour Lou was to take up position. On his left ring finger, Biddy wore a gold band that looked heavy enough to sink an aircraft carrier. Biddy's wife was a stunner. Of course. Swedish blonde with the kind of figure that caught a man's eye like a fishhook. Rafe never let himself look more than a second at a time. Biddy wasn't the kind of man whose wife you wanted to be caught goggling at.

Biddy backed against the desk and folded his arms across his chest. He thought for a beat, then knelt in front of Rafe. The two men looked straight into each other's eyes without expression. Biddy's short hair had a wet look from something he'd rubbed into it. He had a faint spicy scent to him. His small moustache looked recently scissor-trimmed. He puckered his lips, briefly ran two fingers down his aquiline nose. Then a small half-smile formed and, just like that, he eased into another character altogether.

"My man Rayford," he said in that smooth Biddy-voice, with an exaggerated Southern drawl. *Raaayfiiiiiid*. Long on the A, and the second R completely silent. Rafe could never detect a true dialect from Biddy's speech; yet, nobody else spoke like he did. The man's speech patterns were ever-changing. Couldn't pin him down, make him one particular person from one particular place. He slid in and out of accents and personas, easy as an eel. Granted, Rafe hadn't ever been far from the city proper. But nobody on any of the vids talked like Biddy. Some of the crew would lapse into Biddy's accent-of-the-day without knowing they were doing it. Or maybe they did know and they were just sucking up.

Rayford. Nobody else called him that, outside of his family. When he'd had a family. He wasn't especially comfortable having anyone refer to him by his proper name. Is that why Biddy did it? Rafe didn't know. With Biddy, you just had to accept it.

And 'just accepting it' wore a person down after awhile. It got old. Closed up on a man like a trap.

"This man been beat on," Biddy said, not turning his head to look at any of the crew. "C'mon now, Sweet 'n Sour. Do I have to ask which of you did the honors?"

The room stayed silent. Each man stared at Biddy. They knew better than to look away, even for an instant. That's how fast your luck could change, how quickly thrown crystal glassware or tchotchkes could send you to the medicos bleeding from a three-inch facial gash. "I told you I didn't want him hurt. Thelan. I made that clear, didn't I? Spelled it out?"

Sour Lou cleared his throat. "Had to be done. He run from us when we called after him."

"Yeah, and maybe he done it because he didn't know who you was. Way you two dressed, you could be a couple of narcos, or vice, or some goddamn federales," Biddy slid his butt back onto the edge of his desk and returned his attention to Rafe. "These men hurt you? You tell me now. Say the word, I will collect the debt."

Rafe shook his head. He cast his eyes down, like he was weighing options. He wished that Biddy's apparent concern for his well-being could bring him some relief from anxiety, but his own body knew better. His skin pumped out a fresh glaze of sweat.

"You believe me, right?" Biddy said. "You know I was going to do right by you. You ain't down here to get your ass beat."

Despite himself, Rafe looked up. "I'm not?"

Biddy cracked his big, shiny grin. "Nah. I was just needing to see your face. You ain't been around in about a minute. I was thinking you took off or somebody caught up with you. I put the word out, trying to see if something happen to you."

"Nah, I'm good."

"You've looked better." Biddy pushed himself up from the desk and leaned over Rafe. "You looking like you ain't been eating right."

Fishing. Here's how it starts. Biddy doing the interview, and Rafe having to be careful with his answers. If he screwed up? Best case scenario, he'd lose out on most—*all!*—of the score. Zeroed out when the whole job had been his idea in the first place! And worst case? If Biddy decided Rafe wasn't loyal, that Rafe was trying to slip out of his control, chew his way out of the trap?

His eyes quivered in their sockets, wanting to go right back to that damn screen again. Rafe resisted.

"You hear from your brother? How's he doing?" Biddy asked, sliding a curtain aside to reveal a small wet bar. He lifted out a couple of glasses and a Burdeos and poured a healthy shot in each, neat. He strolled back over with the drinks. "Last time I talked to him, he said you ain't been coming around so much."

Rafe took a swallow of the tequila and let his tongue swirl around another before answering. "I want to. I want to go," he said. "They make it hard, visiting. Eyeball you the whole time. I totalled my car, too, so I have to get rides. Not too many people are willing to give you a couple hours of road time and then wait half the day to see somebody."

"That's your brother, though, Rayford." *Raayfiid.* "That's Joseph. It ain't easy, but you got to make it happen. You can't leave him up there thinking he's alone in this world."

"Well—maybe he is," Rafe said, wondering where Biddy was going with this.

Biddy sat in front of Rafe again, and polished off about half of his shot. "I don't forget one of my crew," he said. "Damn fool thing, going out on his own like that. I don't tell you not to do it, y'know?" Biddy's eyes bright as blades, fixed on Rafe. Rafe crossed his legs, realized he looked like some damn prissy woman sitting like that, and uncrossed them. That keen edge to Biddy's look—the man had to know that Rafe was up to some other job, something outside the crew. And, sure, Biddy never *said* the guys couldn't run other jobs on their own. But he'd seen some of the guys who had. He'd seen them in the pit. He'd crammed what was left of their bodies into sacks and hauled them out to the river.

"Problem is," Biddy continued, "when a score goes bad—and it can go bad—best be prepared for it. I told your brother not to sell those guns. Best stay with the tried and true. Stay under my tent, sell my gear, where I tell you to. He learned the hard way.

"But I ain't forgot him. You remember that. I got people up there taking care of him. He don't have to look over his shoulder in the shower, worried someone gonna shove something in him, got it? And that service does not come cheap, Rayford. I'm footing that bill. Biddy watches out for his people."

Sour Lou coughed suddenly into his fist, and wiped the back of his hand across his lips. Biddy stared at the man. "I told you take care of that business, didn't I?" he asked. "Get yourself some damned medicine."

"How much longer we gonna be?" Lou thrust his shoulders against the wall and rapped the paint with his knuckles.

"As long as I say to stay. You leave when I tell you leave." Biddy gave Rafe an exasperated look and shook his head. "I sure do miss your brother. I never got so much as a word of back talk with that man. You see what I got to put up with? Talent has dried the fuck up. I'm left with people don't know how to keep they mouth closed or show a man who pays they salary RESPECT."

"I'd just kind of like to know," Lou replied. "It's been a long day, chasing this fool around half the city. To listen to you chumming around with him, after all the crap, I dunno. Makes me sleepy." He yawned loudly, stretching his arms up before grabbing his elbow and doing a stretch behind his head. Rafe pressed back against his chair. He rested his hands on his lap like he was protecting his scrotum. He couldn't imagine talking like that to Biddy. So casual. Like Biddy had dopey little Chihuahuas down in the hole.

Biddy closed his eyes, then lifted a pant leg. A sickly hum buzzed low in Rafe's head. It was a sound of fear.

"See these leather shoes, Louis?" Biddy asked. "Know what animal they're made from?"

"I dunno—rattlesnake?"

"Three toughest hides to make shoes from: elephant, rhino, hippo. I own all three kinds. You know why?"

"'Cause you need them to kick my ass, I guess." Lou smirked. Rafe's gaze crawled to the monitor. The volume was turned way down, but he thought he heard something. A distant clank, like a heavy chain in motion. At the very edge of the screen, something large and dark slid past the camera. Rafe drew back. It made him think of the glossy side of a gigantic snake slipping past, but in such extreme close-up that he couldn't tell what the thing really was before it vanished off the left side of the monitor.

"No," Biddy said, infinitely patient. "It's so after I bury my goddamn foot deep inside your ass, when I pull it out there's going to enough shoe left to help me stomp every one of your snaggle teeth out of your jaw. Gonna need a mop when I'm through with you."

There were other men in the shadows, but Rafe made no effort to look around or indicate in any way that Biddy wasn't the most interesting man in the room. There was no sound for a few beats save the hiss of cool air from the vents. It was as if each man had sucked in a collective breath and held it. Even Sour Lou looked alarmed now, his face drawn tense, his mouth sucking on itself.

"My father—I ever tell any of you this?" Biddy asked. "My father is from down South. Way down South. South of the border and then keep going till you hit jungle. Anyway, there's a son-bitch you don't run your lip on. You shit out two words he don't wanna hear, and he make you into a pair of shoes. Except he wears boots. Cowboy boots. And I'm not lying, no cow leather or naugahyde. One hundred percent tanned, oiled and stitched together dead hombre. On his feet. And he got a lot of boots, Lou." Biddy smiled, lips tight against his teeth. "He did tell me Anglo skin make a pretty shitty boot. Might use that fat skull of yours for an ashtray though."

The room was dead silent. Rafe couldn't enjoy Sour Lou's sick face. Biddy would soon enough turn that stare back on Rafe. He tried to remember a vid he'd watched way back. Some movie. An old boy had snuck in a bomb and didn't want these aliens to know what was up so he could blow them to hell. Problem was, they could read minds. So he kept telling himself to picture a stone wall so he wouldn't give up his secret. Except they started picking at the wall in his mind, one block at a time. So it was a race to see if they could knock out the wall before—

"We got some real business to take care. Sweet, come get your twin sister and get the fuck out of my office." Biddy suddenly sounded tired, irritated in a way Rafe hadn't heard before. "All ya'll, get out of here now. Thelan, you stay. Bin, you too."

He motioned toward the back of the room. A muscular Asian man, like a Hmong Mr. Universe, was soon on Rafe's left, Thelan on the right. "Rest of you, out. Sour, I want you outside, watching my cars. On the steps. No breaks."

They waited until the room was clear before starting again. Rafe knew what was coming. Serious talk. Business time with Biddy. And his gut knotted up. What had he been thinking about, a wall or something?

"Rayford. I need you to come back to work for me. You see why. Just another demonstration of what total dipshits are working here."

Rafe cleared his throat. "Where'd everybody go? All the other guys? Carmelo, Tony Ritt?"

"Where you think? Guys get killed. Guys like Joseph get careless, go to prison. People leave town and don't tell you. Try to work their own angle so they can get enough cash to leave town and never say a word."

Rafe's gut lurched, made an audible rumbling. He seriously wondered if he was going to crap his pants, right here in the man's HQ. How much did Biddy know? Everything?

Biddy's face was solemn. "I need you to work the corners for me again. I need you to start tomorrow."

Rafe drank the last of his tequila and set the glass on the desk in front of him. He was quiet, trying to figure out the words without tipping anything off. Even though he had a bad feeling it was no use going through the motions to hide anything. "I maybe could next week, Biddy," he said. "I got some business to take care of tomorrow and the next couple days. But I could sling for you first of next week."

"No. I said tomorrow. When I say tomorrow, I mean tomorrow. You think I sent those boys to find you tonight just so I could get a body for next week? Business is hurting, Rayford. You work for me and I'm calling you in. Tomorrow, you're going to be in northeast and you're going to be selling for me, and I'm not going to hear any more no's."

Rafe's face felt clammy. He tried to keep his voice flat and cool, but the alcohol, instead of calming him, was taking him down the paranoia path. What did Biddy know? Oh shit.

A dark shape lunged across the screen with such abrupt and violent energy that Rafe jerked back. The thing—the dog?—was gone again before Rafe got any kind of look at it. The other men—his fellow *crew*, Rafe thought bitterly—laughed uneasily. Biddy cast around a curled smile and a look of mingled excitement and contempt and reached with one hand to flick up the volume.

Caterwauling again. A long and loud wail from the basement holding pens, offscreen.

Rafe shut his eyes briefly. Against his eyelids, he saw the North Carolina he'd imagined. Vaguely green and leafy, nice houses in the secured areas. Sweet tea. He liked sweet tea. Plenty of synthheads and peelfreaks down in the core, plenty to sling to. A market.

Over the audio feed, more howls. Barks that quickly degenerated into furious snarls. Jaws that shut with the springy snap of steel traps. More chains clanked. It was like a damned haunted house down there. Men's voices, low underneath all the noise.

"The thing—the thing is, Biddy, is," Rafe stammered. He tilted his head back, swiveled his eyes upward, and saw that Thelan was now positioned behind him. This was not cool. Not cool at all. "I've got this other thing. I have to do it. You know I want to say no. To the other stuff, not to you! But—I mean—I could really, you know. I could be, like, killed if I don't—"

"Killed by who? Owen Richter?" Biddy made a *pfft* sound with his lips.

Rafe sat still, stunned at hearing the name. He didn't want to believe it. He and Owen just had the meeting last night. Who ratted? How could Biddy know? His thoughts swam inside his brain. *No, no, no . . .*

"Let's get serious, Rayford. No more bullshit." Biddy opened a desk drawer and pulled out a handgun. He slid a magazine inside and pulled back the slide, chambering a round. "I thought about bringing Owen in here, too, and the three of us have a chat, for old time's sake. And the more I thought about it, the more I thought how pissed off I was going to get. And how Owen was going to end up in a ice chest on my boat this weekend off Cape May, and me using parts of him to try and catch stripers and mako. What a goddamn waste of time, for all of us.

"So let's cut to the chase. Word's out that you and Richter got a job that's gonna get you all mixed up with one of the execution companies. Regency."

God—no—

"I don't fuck with those guys, Rayford. And I don't permit any of my crew to fuck with them neither."

Frustration tore through Rafe's veins. He realized he was twisting in his chair, like some chained animal crazy at the weight dragging around its legs. Chains like these, a man couldn't run, couldn't even walk. Could barely crawl across the dirt, for fuck's sake.

"Point A." Biddy tipped a finger. "Most of those execution company guys are former military PTSD psy-co-paths. Trained to kill your ass. Like ninjas. Bruce Lee shit. And Biddy respects that." Biddy grinned. "Point B, we are all in the same game, Rayford. Those psycho guys—they got plenty of shit in their heads they want to make go away. And they got plenty of cash to pay for what we're slinging that's gonna do the job for them. Biddy makes money from them. I'm already at that table. Why I wanna mess that up?"

"I guess—I don't—know," Rafe stammered.

"Why I wanna let some moron from my crew mess that up? We all about the money out here. My businesses respect theirs. We our own chambers of commerce. I go down to Regency, to Eye for Eye, to Elite, I go down there to sell. I can't have my people messing shit up! That makes me look bad! Am I getting through to you?"

Rafe nodded slowly, still in a daze. He'd almost had all that money. Almost. His life story, in a nutshell. If they ever made a vid about him, that should be the title. *Almost*. He was going to leave here even poorer than before because now Biddy'd taken all the hope away too. Wrapped those chains tighter.

Hell, the way Biddy was waving that gun around, maybe Rafe wasn't leaving at all.

"The one thing—the one thing!—in your favor, is I take it you wanted to be straight up on this, right?" Biddy asked. "Am I right?"

Rafe heard the click of a blade opening behind him. Thelan. Bin was resting a hand on his shoulder, giving him a squeeze beyond supportive, like he was palpating tendon. Biddy slipped in front of the desk again. He leaned against it and raised his leg, putting his rhino-leather shoe—was it only rhino?—against Rafe's chest.

"You and Richter cooked this up, right? Angles. Thought them all through, did you? Uh-huh. Right. Let me tell you something, Rayford. You and Richter were going to get so blown away. But lucky for you, I'm here and I am ready to save your asses."

Confused, Rafe gawked at the man. What was Biddy saying? That he was going to let Rafe go through with the job? After all that talk about psychokillers and ninjas?

"It's okay," Rafe said. "We got this. Owen and me, we worked this all out—"

"If I didn't care about my crew, I would just let it all happen. You and Richter and whatever chumps he's got to back you up. But I let you do this thing by yourselves, it'd be—" Biddy spread his hands in a question and looked behind Rafe. "What'd you call it, Thelan?"

"Criminal negligence," Thelan replied. Rafe felt the knife blade press against his ear and upper jaw. His pulse ticked along at a fast clip back there, near the hinge of his jaw. Biddy pressed his shoe deeper into Rafe's chest.

"Plus, when I got to tell somebody I told you so, all the somebodies will be dead and I got nobody to talk to. So, this is your lucky day, Rayford. Biddy's gonna bail your ass out once again. I've got an idea gonna be win-win all the way around."

Win-win? Well, that was the kiss of death, Rafe thought. The job with Owen was gone to shit. No *almost* about it.

More yowling and a steady, nerve-grinding whine came over the audio feed. The noise antagonized the migraine starting up behind Rafe's eyes.

Biddy stood and swept his palms against each other like he was about to tidy things up. He shut off the feed, video and audio. The screen went black. The sudden quiet practically massaged Rafe's temples. He shut his eyes for a moment, leaning into the silence. He had to face facts here. Either the score wasn't going down at all or, if it was, Rafe wasn't going to see a dime from it. Forget North Carolina. Goodbye, Charlotte. Adios, Virginia Beach.

But he couldn't stop himself from begging. "Biddy." Rafe's voice was a child's. He could have slapped himself for sounding like such a weasel. "Please, you got to let us do this—I need the money, man. I—if it gets watered down any more than it is, I'm—I got debts, I'm getting crushed, they got eyes on me all day and night—

"You're using the old math, Rayford. The one you made the mistake with. The old math that said you and Owen could pull the thing off. You was figuring on getting a fifty-fifty, but half of nothing still's nothing. Plus, you'd get your ass blown away, and well, now we in the negatives. So throw all that out. It's time for the new math."

Biddy Math. Goddamn it.

Biddy pulled Rafe to his feet and slung an arm around his shoulders, laughing like the old times. In spite of the popping of his dream bubble, Rafe couldn't help feeling a little better. Biddy had him almost cradled in his arms, and the sound of his happiness infected Rafe. Like they'd just been out on the town, hitting the Philly nightclubs and strip joints, on Biddy's expense account, and they were just getting home. He wasn't just on a Biddy crew. He was the leader of a Biddy crew. And Biddy would take good care of him.

Wouldn't he?

Biddy hooked a thumb toward Bin. "Bin. Go get our newest acquisition ready to meet Rayford."

Rafe's head jolted upright. His heart crammed into his throat. He hadn't heard that right. Had he? Biddy didn't just say—

Bin slipped away to the stairs and Rafe's memories of the fun times with Biddy and the crew slipped away just as fast. Suddenly, all he could see was the pit. All he could hear was the hum of the wires and the howls of the man jouncing against them. The stink of dog fur and piss jammed up his nostrils.

Biddy forced Rafe's head down against his shoulder again, kept Rafe locked there while the elevator quietly whirred up the shaft to the top floor.

"C'mon." Biddy gave Rafe a shove—not too hard, might be friendly, might not—and then they were all in the elevator, heading down. Rafe's stomach sank faster than the cab. He glimpsed himself in the mirrored wall. He looked like a dead man already. Face drawn tight, cheeks hollowed out, eyes big and staring out like hunted animals watching for the predator fast approaching. His muscles were so stiff, his body so rigid, he was surprised he didn't topple over.

The elevator chimed when it reached the basement. Rafe wanted to stick right there, stick his feet to the floor and ride that elevator forever. But as soon as the door slid open, Biddy and the crew pushed through the gap like a rip tide. Rafe stumbled along with the current.

They left the elevator, pivoted, and for a moment Rafe stopped in front of those stairs leading deeper down into the darkness. But Biddy wasn't having any hesitation. "Let's go!" Biddy's voice was electric with energy. He sounded happy. Excited. Just like during the good times. Yeah, and also just like when he watched something getting ripped to bloody pieces in the hole.

Biddy grabbed Rafe by the arm and tugged him onto the steps, down into the sub-basement and then lower. The air grew colder as they descended. Goosebumps exploded up and down Rafe's arms. Barking erupted from the shadows at the far end of the room. The smell from the dog pens rolled over Rafe in a flood of odors: blood, shit, animal breath reeking across yellow teeth.

Rafe had a moment of pure terror in front of the pit. Biddy was going to pitch him down into the dirt and animal dung. Introduce him to the new dogs, all right.

"Get the lights!" Biddy crowed. Thelan hit a switch which lit up the pit. Nothing in there. Not yet. "Hey Bin! Bin! Bring him out front here so we can see this magnificent bastard," Biddy shouted, resting his elbows on the observation railing. He nudged Rafe, and nodded toward two shapes approaching them just out of the light. Two large shadows. Hmong Mr. Universe, struggling to hold onto a strap latched to a harness around something, something that walked on four legs and had paws, but was not quite like anything Rafe had ever laid eyes on before. A dog, of some bizarre kind. Somehow mixed with a bear? But no, he could make out the cropped ears atop its head, the stub of a cropped tail.

Rafe had seen many a pitbull locked in a death struggle down there while men screamed from the sidelines and thousands of dollars changed hands. But this was no pitbull. It smelled different somehow, more wild. More dangerous. Every cell in Rafe's body recoiled from the odor. He glanced back over at the stairs.

Biddy gave the widest smile Rafe had ever seen on the man's face. "Rayford, meet your guarantee," Biddy said. "You take this bad boy with you, I guarantee, not only you make the score, but you live to tell. Now, what you got here is a loaner, but I know your credit good. Anyway, Bin comes with the deal, to make sure nothing goes wrong."

Rafe stared as the beast entered the pit below. Bin was obviously leaning back with all his strength, and still the animal was coming forward. The hairs on the back of Rafe's neck sprang up.

"What is that thing?" he finally managed to ask.

"Riker's Doberman. Hellhound. Oh, yeah, I see you heard of 'em."

"I've heard of them, but . . . damn." Rafe couldn't stop gawking at the monster.

"Got this straight from the Cortez cartel. Bred right in their own labs in Baja. Cost me a fortune, but what a weapon, huh? Got venom in its spit, you know that? Nerve toxins, serious shit. Truth. His name's Bae."

The massive creature paused. Its enormous head swiveled to look up at Rafe. The yellow eyes blazed. Rafe shrank back. This thing? Out on the streets in Philly?

"I—I dunno," he stammered. "It's really nice of you, Biddy, but you just said, the thing cost a fortune. I can't afford to pay you for that kind of loaner."

"Sure you can. Between your take on this job with Owen, plus double my usual percentage for the slinging you're doing for me rest of the month." He gave Rafe a slap on the back. "We're good."

Rafe plus job equals zero. Biddy Math.

Biddy slapped a hand happily on the rail and turned to go back up the stairs.

One last chance. "But Biddy!" Rafe called out. The Hellhound lasered its attention on Rafe as if attracted by the quaver in his voice. The beast swelled toward him, the muscles in its shoulders bulging. The coarse fur on its neck stood up like quills. Bin's enormous arms bulged too as he leaned back, using all his weight to counteract the dog's pull.

Biddy paused to look back over his shoulder.

"This thing . . . this animal. I won't be able to control it," Rafe said. Admitting to weakness. It was pathetic and Rafe knew it, but what else could he do? Pity and contempt shone in Biddy's eyes. "It gets away, out there on the streets? What if it kills somebody, some . . . some kid? We won't be able to just walk away from that, Biddy. That's a murder rap."

Even though Rafe said 'we', he knew that, in reality, he was in this mess alone. If he went down, Biddy wasn't about to go down with him.

"You gotta stop worrying so much," Biddy said. "Bin'll help you get used to him. Right, Bin?"

"Sure thing," Bin grunted, straining against the animal.

"Little Hellhound's gonna help Rafe hit the score on this one. Bae's gonna eat gourmet tonight!" Biddy sang out and loosed the laugh that could bring down a room.

Rafe wasn't feeling it, though. He looked away from Biddy, down into the pit. Bin was losing ground, obviously overmatched by pure animal muscle. How this guaranteed anything, how this was going to work out on the street, when it counted, he'd have to figure out later. They'd have to figure it out. Owen wouldn't budge on his cut, and Biddy had given his terms. All that was leftover for Rafe was—hell, Rafe couldn't finish the sentence.

"All right," Thelan called across from the other side of the room, near the pens. "You heard the boss. Let's get things movin'." He flicked a switch and most of the lights went out. Shadows swam in the pit. "Bin, take the Riker's out through the death door. Me and Rafe'll meet you out there with one of the vans."

No more barking or howling, just snorting, and deep, powerful gusts of breath. Whatever this beast really was, it was sucking all the energy out of Rafe. A true force of nature. Bin was dragging at it like a bull, and the Hellhound—What was its name? Bae?—only lurched backward a quarter inch at a time. At this rate, it was going to take half the night to get Bae to the back exit where the dog fight losers and Biddy's torn-up enemies were carted out after an evening's entertainment.

"C'mon, Rafe!" Bin yelled, sweat glittering on his face in the dimness. "Get your ass down here and help!" With an enormous heave, Bin got the creature to scrabble back another inch. Its head still tilted up and its stare never wavered away from Rafe who stood frozen against the railing as if he might never move from that spot for the rest of his life.

He felt dizzy. Was the pit growing larger? Opening wider, spreading out into the shadows? And there at the heart of it: a pair of glittering eyes, black lips curled around fangs that dripped a steady stream of drool, and a growl like a chainsaw that tore Rafe right down to the core.

EMERALD CITY

I ALMOST RAN AWAY LAST SUMMER, and the summer before that. But this time, it's for real. This time, I have the money.

Okay, I *will* have the money.

I'd been outside all day hanging with Mateo and the twins. We took turns on the scooter Mateo's cousins fixed up for him and kept an eye on Mr. Jennings' house across the street. It was hot, almost a hundred out, and the concrete burned through the bottom of my sneakers. My hair stuck to my neck and glued itself to my scalp. There wasn't any wind at all so even when I took off my t-shirt, all I did was sweat.

I was thirsty, but I waited to go inside until my mouth was so dry I couldn't stand it anymore. I went around to the back of the house to the kitchen door. I'd make this a quick stop and right back outside.

I don't like spending a lot of time in there.

The A/C's broken so all the doors and windows were propped open. The last guy that lived with us ripped the kitchen screen door half off its hinges and it was still hanging sideways onto the porch. I high-stepped over it and into the kitchen.

My mom and Mr. Cave-Man Number Three leaned against the counter in front of the sink. He was wrapped around her and she grinned at me over his hairy shoulder and waved her hand around to show something silver sparkling in and out like tinsel around one of her fingers. "Guess what, Patros?" She half-sang the words.

I stopped dead and stared at them. Again, huh? This is what she did every single time. Brought the guy into the house and then married him later if she could get him to say okay. My mom's been married five times.

She ran her fingers along the cave man's jaw. His skin was all bristly with whiskers, like somebody'd dumped a shaker full of pepper over his face. Mom giggled and winked at me. Her eyelashes were gummy and thick, like black goo. The skin under her eyes was blue and papery. She and the cave man had been up most of the night. I could hear them from where I slept on the living room floor. Mom had the only bedroom in the place.

"What d'you think?" she asked and stuck her hand out. The ring looked like a piece of foil twisted into a circle. "We're doing the deed tomorrow. You can come down to City Hall with us. Be the best man." She giggled again. That sound ate at me, made me pull in my shoulders and look away. Like a bird choking on something stuck in its throat.

"Okay," I said to the floor. Sunlight blasted through the open doorway, made crumbs glow on the tiles.

"Naaahhhh," the cave man said. He didn't sound like a bird. He sounded more like a goat gargling that one word on and on. "Naaahh. Joe's the best man. We don't need any kids around for it."

Mom clumped her sticky eyelashes together for a minute, looking at him, then looking at me. "You'll like that, won't you, Patros? You can stay here, play with your friends all day. And just think. By tomorrow night, you'll have a new dad. All official. Won't you like that?" Her little bird voice begging me to say how much I loved all this. What a great guy he was. What a good job she'd done picking him.

And right that second, I knew that this time I was really going to do it. Leave her and the furry beast guy and run off to the emerald city.

I nodded at her—don't let her think anything's wrong—turned around, ran right out across the back porch and around the side of the house to the street. My throat felt all shriveled up. I'd drink whatever was left in Mateo's bottle. Backwash, whatever, I didn't care.

Because I was out of here.

The emerald city. Grownups never talked about it, just us kids. I'd find it. I *had* to. Because Mom's boyfriends and husbands and "special friends" got worse every time and this guy wasn't going to be any different.

Last week he'd shoved me against the fridge for "disrespecting" him. Pushed me so hard all the cereal boxes and crackers toppled down on my head. He hadn't given me any black eyes yet, no cracked tooth or arm yellow with bruises, but that shove told me everything I needed to know.

Here's some things I've heard about the emerald city.

That the kids who go there when they're still young? Like five or six? They get stuck on short. Never grow over four feet. On account of all the weird chemicals that are still in the dirt and stuck on every doorknob and window and table and chair like blobs of invisible bubble gum. But I'm already over five-foot even though I'm only ten. I don't care about being short anyway.

I heard that they built a giant castle out of boards and hoods and doors and glass they took from all the cars and houses that got left behind after the government made everybody leave and built the fence. I heard that every kid has their own room in the castle, and at the very top is a swimming pool made of windshields duct-taped together. They let it fill up with rain and they float in it all summer long and stare up at the clouds. The reason we can't see the castle from the fence is because it's way, way deep inside, right at the very middle of the no-go zone.

I heard they catch water in old trash cans and it turns their tongues silver when they drink it. That one *could* be true because it works that way with freezer pops and grape jolly ranchers. And they grow potatoes and carrots that are as big as an arm—that's because of all the weird chemicals in the dirt—and strawberries that are red, *really* red, like blood and they have a big feast every night with a bonfire. Oh, yeah, and they eat dog-meat, cat-meat, raccoon-meat and squirrel.

I could eat a cat, no problem. As long as it was cooked.

Fuzzy and Faro, the McGrath twins, told me they were standing next to the fence one night when it was just getting dark and they could see some of those emerald city kids through the wire. The kids were running in and out of the buildings, ducking down behind the skeleton cars, and they'd stop every once in a while and dart out and throw a spear at something and then jump around and holler. Fuzzy said they were just shadows, all dark, and you couldn't really see anything particular about them, but Faro said they wore loin-cloths.

Why would they be wearing loin-cloths when there has to be a ton of old clothes left in closets and dressers all over the zone?

Faro. What a moron.

But you know what's the best thing about the emerald city?

No moms.

No boyfriends.

No stepdads.

But here's the thing. They won't let you in unless you bring some money with you. It might be a hundred dollars. It might be five hundred. I'm not sure. I've heard different things. But you have to pay it because there are some things they can't grow in there for themselves, or hammer together out of scraps, or find in the empty houses.

Like medicine that isn't twenty years gone bad. Like batteries that aren't crusted-over and dead. Like ammunition.

A couple of the older kids who I don't think would lie about it said that they've seen emerald city kids at the quick shop. Said the kids come creeping in sideways, eyes clicking around every direction, hair long and wild. They go flickering up and down the aisles, fast, grabbing the batteries, grabbing the codeine and the advil and band-aids and toothpaste. And they dump everything on the counter by the register and never say a word.

And they always pay in cash.

Money was the big reason I never tried running before. Things were already bad at my house and not getting any better. Last year was Cave Man Number Two and the year before that was Mr. Chicken Legs. Mom's husbands always grabbed and pushed and hit. Hit her and me and whatever stepkids happened to be living with us. My stepbrothers and sisters changed all the time. They came and went, there one week, gone the next, then back again. I ignored them. At least Mateo and the twins stayed put. You could count on them being around.

I'm done with staying put. As soon as I have my hands on the money, I'm gone. Through the fence and into the zone, all the way into its heart, and I'm never coming back.

I scurried along the dirt path worn between my house and the boarded-up place next door, and shot out to the street. The sidewalk on my block was a rubbly mess, all cracked up and broken, so I trotted down the middle of the street. It was dead, not a car moving along it.

Mateo was sitting in a strip of dirt between the street and the sidewalk with a sandwich gripped in one hand and a big bottle of punch drink in the other. A corner of orange cheese curled over the bottom slice of bread and lettuce squeezed out onto his fingers. Cold water drops slid down the plastic bottle. I pushed my tongue around my mouth and stared.

Mateo saw me staring and pushed the drink toward me.

"Thanks." I dropped onto the dirt beside him and took a long drink. The cold punch was heaven going down my throat. Down at the corner, the twins tried to lasso a hubcap with a jump rope. Their little sister stood next to them and cried, just like always. I handed the drink back to Mateo and started eyeing the sandwich. He pushed that at me next.

"Thanks," I mumbled again, through a mouthful of bologna and cool, damp lettuce. He didn't ask why I hadn't gotten any food of my own when I was inside. I told him, "My mom and the new guy were all over each other."

"Gross."

"Yeah." I took another big bite of Mateo's sandwich, chewed, swallowed. "They're getting married. Tomorrow." I handed the sandwich back.

"*Gross,*" he said again. Because what else was there to say about that?

Except—

"I'm leaving."

Mateo didn't need to ask where. I'd only talked about the emerald city about a million times. He pointed out the one problem with my plan: "But we didn't get any money yet."

He leaned back on his elbows and stared at the house straight across the street from us. I stared at it too.

It was a shoebox house, like every other house on the street, with a tiny front yard and crumbling steps.

Weeds and vines grew over everything like they were trying to eat the concrete. There was only enough room on the front porch for one chair, a wooden one that looked like it would give you about a hundred splinters in your butt if you sat on it. One of the windows was missing a couple of panes. Green curtains sagged against it on the inside so you couldn't see anything in there.

"You think he's dead?" I asked. "I haven't seen him in, what?" I counted on my fingers, squinted against the sun. "Four days?" I had no idea how old Mr. Jennings was but he looked ancient. All withered and white and creeping along with a pair of canes. He lived by himself.

Mateo gave me the last of the punch. I rolled the wet cool of the bottle back and forth across my forehead before I drank down the rest of it.

"Does it matter?" he said. "I mean, as long as nobody knows he's dead. As long as his daughter doesn't know, she'll still come here looking for him, right?"

I thought about that. He was right. As long as the old man's daughter, Tori, thought he was alive, there was a chance she'd show up here. And that was all that mattered because if we saw her and sent a message to the guys who'd asked us to watch for her, then they were going to give us money.

Going to give me and Mateo money, at least. I made a visor out of my hand and squinted down the street. Fuzzy and Faro had given up on the lasso and were spinning pebbles around inside the hubcap and screaming at their little sister every time she stepped on the hubcap and made it stop. She'd made a belt out of her muddy jump rope and was sucking on one end of it.

The twins were stupid enough that they hadn't asked for money. They could be bought off for a couple bags of candy—that's what they'd asked for if you can believe it, chocolate bars and jolly ranchers and gum. Their little sister seemed to think she was going to get some Baby-Go-Potty doll out of the deal even though the men hadn't said one word about her being in on any of it.

"But what if she never shows up?" I said. I leaned forward, hunching over my knees and picking at dead skin on my big toe. I couldn't help worrying. "What if those guys find her somewhere else first?"

Mateo shrugged. "Then that's how it goes."

With a sudden, hard jerk, I tore off a strip of skin. Too much skin. What was left underneath was red and tender. It hurt when I touched it.

Things were different for Mateo. He didn't have his dad either, but his mom was all right and so was the aunt who lived with them. He had grown-up brothers and sisters, and all those big cousins too, hanging out, stopping by, watching out for him. What did I have? Cave Man Number Three, that's what I had.

"I need that money." My voice sounded squeezed. "You know I've got to have it, for the emerald city." I let my eyes squeeze way down too, until Mr. Jennings' house was a thin gray line shimmering across the middle of my eyes. "What if she never comes here? What if we never even get a chance?"

Where else was I going to get anything like a hundred dollars? I couldn't even steal it from my mom or the Cave Man. They both used money chips. There was never any cash sitting around. My brain scrambled, trying to come up with some other possible source, but there wasn't any. Not for that amount.

My stomach crumpled up on itself, like a paper bag balled up and thrown in the trash. I couldn't breathe. What if I had to just stay here and wait and wait until Cave Man Number Three decided I needed a belt across the face?

I swung sideways, grabbed Mateo's arm. My eyes were wide open now and I got my face so close to his that I think I spat on him a little when I talked.

"I *need* the money, Mat." I sounded a little wild, maybe, or maybe it was the spit, but Mateo pulled back a little and worked his arm loose. "I need it today."

He shook his head. "What do you want me to do? I can't make that Tori lady appear—" He snapped his fingers. "Like that."

Suddenly I knew. I knew exactly what we had to do. I jumped up and reached for his arm again, practically hauled him onto his feet.

"What?" he said. "What?"

"You've got the comm on you right now?" I asked. I didn't have to explain *which* comm. He knew I meant the loaner the two guys told him to use to let them know the second that Mr. Jennings' daughter showed up.

"Yeah." He pulled it out of his front pocket and frowned at me like I was crazy for even suggesting he might not have it on him at all times, just in case.

"Tell them she's here."

Mateo stared at me. "What?"

"Just say we saw her."

"Are you crazy?"

"Are you stupid?" I answered. "You're going to let the money get away from us?" I made a grab for the comm, but Mateo twisted sideways, snugging it against his chest with both hands.

"Okay, Einstein, and then what do we do when they show up and find out she's not really here? You want to be the one to piss them off?"

But my brain was humming. I had an answer ready. "We say she was inside for, like, two minutes and then she left. And we make up what direction she went. And that's it. They go look for her. They won't know it's a lie. How would they?"

The plan unspooled in my head. It was smooth and perfect, from the time Mateo sent the message on the comm to the moment my fingers closed around the money. Excitement fizzed in my chest. We should have done this the first day. What had we been waiting for? Talk about stupid.

Mateo flicked his gaze down to the corner where the twins and their little sister were playing Infected, chasing each other down the street, in and out around parked cars, screaming like little maniacs.

"What about them?" Mateo asked.

The fizzing in my chest suddenly went flat. Yeah, what about them? They were too young and too dumb to be trusted with a lie. They'd tell on us to the two men without even knowing that's what they were doing. And then what? No money, for sure. But maybe worse. The men had acted really friendly and nice to us, but would they still be nice if they knew we were trying to pull one over? The one guy had been really big, with huge hands that would make huge fists. The skin on his knuckles had looked red and rough, like it had been scraped halfway off.

But Caveman Number Three had big fists too, and there wasn't really any doubt at all that he'd be using them on me eventually. Better to take a risk. Get that money.

"How about—" My brain scrambled. "Do you have *any* money at all?"

Mateo eyed me. Suspicious. "Maybe. A little. How much are you talking about?"

"Just enough to get them out of here for a few minutes. Down to the store to buy a popsicle or something. We can say we saw her while they were gone."

"I'm not buying those idiots a popsicle!"

"Shh!" I cut a glance down the street—Faro had climbed on top of one of the cars and was drumming on its roof. Fuzzy danced in the street, throwing himself around like a crazy person. I drew in close to Mateo. "It's an investment, see? You put a little bit of money in, but you get a whole lot more out."

Mateo looked skeptical. "I don't know."

"Come on, Mateo!" Forget convincing him. I was going for flat-out begging now. "I need your help, man! You want me to get beat up again?" I twisted my arm so the underside between the elbow and shoulder was practically in his face. There was a puckery scar, three inches long, from the time Mr. Chicken Legs shoved me against a shelf and the sharp metal edge caught me on the arm and sliced me up. Twenty stitches.

Mateo's face got all tight and weird when he looked at my scar. After a while he said, "Okay. But when we get the money, you have to pay me back for three popsicles."

Five minutes later, the McGrath kids were gone, headed down to the quick shop for bomb pops and fudgesicles. All three of them were too dumb to wonder why Mateo had suddenly gotten so generous.

Mateo sent a message on the comm the minute the twins vanished around the corner. The response was instant: "On my way."

Mateo and I stared at each other.

"My?" I said. "Just one of them's coming?" I didn't know if that was good news or bad. Maybe they weren't taking us seriously, thought this was probably a false alarm or something. I wondered if the one guy who showed up would even bother bringing cash with him.

He had to. He *had* to.

Mateo crossed to the old man's house and sat down on the curb to wait. I paced up the sidewalk to the corner, turned around and walked back down the block. Did it again.

I was coated in sweat. Wished I could have one of those popsicles, too. I crossed the street and dropped down next to Mateo. "How long's it been?"

He looked at the comm. "Fifteen minutes."

"Feels like fifteen hours."

"Maybe nobody'll come." Mateo's face brightened at the thought.

I jumped back up and started pacing again, on the twenty feet of ground-up sidewalk in front of the old man's house. "They'd better come is all I have to say."

Mateo frowned up at me. The sun was going down but it was still bright, a knife over my shoulder, making his eyes swim like black water.

"I'm thinking this was a bad idea, Patros."

I stared down at him and didn't say anything.

He raised the comm for a second and said, "It's not too late. I can send them another message. Tell them we made a mistake. Not to come."

I threw a wild look up the street to the house where right now the Cave Man and my mom were probably doing it in her bedroom or maybe right there in the kitchen where I'd left them for all I knew. Wouldn't be the first time.

"You can't do that. Mateo. Please."

He shrugged, shifted his butt around on the concrete. Wouldn't meet my eyes. "I just have a bad feeling, that's all."

I spread my hands out. "Are you afraid of them?"

Now his chin shot up and he looked square at me. "Hell, yeah."

"I didn't think they seemed so bad." Was I lying? I don't think so. They'd seemed like guys who could get kind of rough if they had to, but not crazy violent. Not wild like the skinwaste drug slingers in the neighborhood, yanking out guns and baseball bats and razors at the drop of a hat. These guys seemed like they were in control of themselves. I liked that. It was predictable. It was smart. It was the opposite of the cave man type who just did whatever stupid thing happened to crawl into his brain.

"Well, still . . ." Mateo brought the comm up like he was about to send another message. I thought about grabbing it, but before I could do anything, a car came slewing around the corner and churned across the chewed-up concrete. It was a huge car, dark red, long as a boat with dark windows and a hood about the size of a football field. The hubcaps were polished and flashing so bright in the sun that they hurt my eyes. Were they real silver? I didn't know, but this sure wasn't any car I'd ever seen before.

The car stopped in front of us, right in the middle of the street in a spot where the pavement didn't look quite so much like an earthquake had cracked it open. The windows were tinted so dark I couldn't even tell how many people were inside.

"Is that one of the same guys?" I whispered to Mateo.

He shook his head slowly, eyes never leaving the car. "I don't think so."

The engine, smooth and quiet, cut out. The sounds that were always around us—blasting tailpipes, the rattling monster rush of the El, vids playing through the open windows of the houses, kids yelling, babies screaming—it seemed like they all fell silent too as soon as that big engine stopped. I didn't hear anything except the deep creak of the driver's door as it swung open.

A black shoe, polished and shiny like the hubcaps, lowered to the street, and then the other shoe. They were fancy shoes like somebody rich and important would wear, somebody on Wall Street or a lawyer or some bigshot in the vids.

The car gave a groan as the driver pulled himself to his feet, hauling himself up by his arms, his hands gripping the top of the open door. He breathed noisily like he was so out of shape it was hard for him to stand up.

I shot Mateo a sideways look—*I told you so!*—and grinned. "Still scared?" I said out of the corner of my mouth.

Mateo grinned back at me.

We had this. We so had the money.

I mean, what the hell was this guy? Nobody we'd seen before. He was big, yeah, very big. But where the other man, the one who'd loaned Mateo the comm, had been tall and muscular, this guy was a tall tub of lard. He was dressed like a businessman, nice black pants and a white shirt, a jacket that he was trying to fight his way out of at the moment. Every part of him wobbled— arms, legs, gut, chins . . . and there were a ton of those. His hair was thin. His skin was a weird kind of grayish-white that made him look like he was sick.

He finally got both arms out of the jacket sleeves. He looked over at me and Mateo, gave a quick little shrug and a closed smile that punched dimples into his fat cheeks. He tossed the jacket behind him without looking over his shoulder. It vanished into the car.

He jelloed his way over to us, picking a path between the rocks and chunks of concrete like he was afraid to get his shoes dirty. He even had a small limp. Mateo and I couldn't stop shooting looks at each other, couldn't stop smiling. How'd we get so lucky?

I closed my eyes just for a second, sent a quick and silent 'thank you' up into the air without moving my lips. I liked to keep that kind of thing to myself.

When the man stopped in front of us, I realized just how huge he really was. He smelled fancy. Cologne, but not the heavy, stinking kind that Mateo's older brothers wore, the kind that always gave me a headache if I was around it for too long. He made a small wheezing sound when he breathed.

"Good afternoon, lads." He sounded funny, halfway like he was from England or something. He stuck out a hand. "Allow me to introduce myself. Mr. Whelk."

I didn't know what to do. Did he want to shake my hand? *My* hand? I'm ten years old. Nobody wants to shake my hand. Then I thought that was actually pretty cool of him. I stuck my hand out too. He didn't shake it, just held it for way too long. I tried to pull my hand away, but he just kept slowly tightening his grip. It hurt. I squinched up my face, jerked at my hand, but he just kept tightening his fingers until I thought he was going to crush the bones.

Mateo stepped forward, frowning. "Hey, Mister, you need to—"

The man—Mr. Whelk—interrupted him, dropping my hand at the same time and staring up at Mr. Jennings' house. "Where is our darling errant girl?"

Now the look Mateo and I gave each other was confused.

"The, the what?" Mateo asked. He'd put both of his hands behind his back, not risking a handshake himself.

At least four chins joggled as the man turned his attention full on Mateo. "Please don't tell me that you have no concept of this endeavor and of your own role within it."

"What?" That seemed to be Mateo's only word now.

"The quarry, the prey, the game, the prize, the plunder," said Mr. Whelk. He peered into Mateo's face and then leaned close to peer into mine. Something cold went through me. His eyes were small and gray, like dead things jammed behind those fat eyelids and the stubby, burnt-looking lashes. He sank back away from me and sighed. "I speak of the damsel in distress, of course, the Executable. Miss Tori Jennings."

"Oh," Mateo and me said at the same time.

"I received your electronic missive at 7:02 p.m. It is now 7:31. You note the speed with which I hastened to your call." He glanced at each of us like he expected an answer. Mateo tossed me a helpless look. Neither one of us knew what the hell to say to this guy.

He let out another long sigh and said, "You sighted her when precisely?"

Mateo just stared, his mouth open. I'd figured he would be a good liar, but I'd figured wrong.

I sent up another little prayer—not even words, just a feeling of desperation flying skyward—and took over. "Right before Mateo sent you the message. We didn't waste any time."

The massive face swung toward me. It was like a planet hurtling toward me, not caring that I was in its way. "No?"

Worry like slivers of glass in my stomach. "No."

"And I assume the sighting occurred on this same charming boulevard on which we now disport ourselves?"

I turned into Mateo's twin. Staring, my mouth open, trying to understand what the man was asking me.

No sigh from him this time, but a quick clicking of his tongue. He turned to nod at Mr. Jennings' house. I had the uneasy feeling that he was somehow finished with us.

"And that is the relevant domicile?"

"The what?" I said.

He stepped to the little broken black gate that was supposed to keep people off Mr. Jennings' front steps. The gate came up to the man's thighs. He leaned forward, jiggled it back and forth a couple of times, let out a yelp of laughter that brought out a fresh coat of sweat all over my body and soaked my t-shirt for about the tenth time that day. It wasn't exactly an out-of-control kind of laugh, but it had a thin border of blood running along the edge. It reminded me of Caveman Number One.

Without any warning, the man wheeled around and flowed toward us. He didn't look wobbly and awkward any more. He moved like a shark through water, a huge shark, faster than I ever would have imagined. And then he stood so close to us, it was like standing in the shadow of a mountain. The shadow was cold.

"Let me put this next question very plainly," he said. "So plainly that even simpletons like you can understand it."

Was that an insult? I thought it was. But I just nodded and nodded. Next to me, Mateo was nodding too, like his head was about to come off.

"My question is this. How could you have seen Miss Jennings here in the heart of Philadelphia less than half an hour ago when other operatives with my company have tracked her to Virginia?"

Beetles crawling in my stomach, that's what it felt like when he stabbed those dead-knife eyes in my direction. I gave a wild glance down the block—don't know what I was thinking. That my mom was going to suddenly come sprinting out the front door of our house and save me? But when I saw that sad, saggy house, I knew I couldn't give up, not with the money so close. This man had money. No question about that.

Mateo blurted out, "We must've made a mistake. We're very sorry, sir."

But I ran right over his words with my own. "No. It's those other people, sir. Those op—operatives. They have to be wrong about Virginia because we just saw her here." I raised one hand flat, palm toward him. "I swear."

For a minute, I thought I had him. I really did. Then another smile pressed into that dough-face of his and he said, "A sworn oath from you carries about the same weight as a pinky promise from my three-year-old niece." The smile stretched and stretched until it was like his laugh earlier.

A little bit bloody, maybe.

His smile stretched until it snapped. And when it snapped shut, it was like a rubber band when it shoots off your fingers. So fast that it's hitting the target before you even see it leave your hand.

He pressed down over me, grabbed my wrist, crushing it. My whole body tightened against the pain. I looked up and saw that he had his other hand around Mateo's wrist with the same kind of grip. Crazy how blubber could hide so much muscle.

"Now. Which of you miscreants sent that message?"

I didn't say anything. Neither did Mateo. The pressure on my wrist increased. Sweat in my eyes, air hissing out between my teeth.

From the corner of my eye, I saw Mateo raise his head. His mouth opened. For a second, I wondered if he was going to bite the guy, but then I realized, no. Mateo was going to say it was all his idea. Take the blame, take whatever punishment this guy handed out. He was that kind of friend.

But so was I.

I shot my head up and said, "I did it."

The man swiveled his head toward me. His gray stare covered me like cold water. Mateo shuffled a couple of steps back, bent over his wrist, rubbing it, and I realized the man had let him go.

This was all going to come down on me. Just me.

The man was bending my wrist back. My eyes stung, hot and wet. I was *not* going to cry. I sucked in my lips, shut my eyes.

The man jerked me to one side, not letting up on his grip one bit. I opened my eyes. He looked at Mateo who stood hunched in the same spot, gawking up at the guy.

"You can thank your friend here," the man told Mateo, "for getting you off easy."

Mateo's glance cut toward me. His eyes were huge, a little wild, his forehead wrinkled. I think he was trying to say he was sorry. For what?

The man told him, "Keep the comm. Keep watching. But if you try this—or anything like this—again, I'll make certain I'm accompanied by a certain favorite colleague next time. He specializes in breaking hands and jaws. He also enjoys leaving a person without teeth. I don't expect you want to meet him. Do you?"

Mateo shook his head. He was staring at the man's gut, not glancing over at me.

"Go home," Mr. Whelk told him.

Mateo turned and ran. I heard his sneakers smack up the front steps of his house. The screen door thwapped shut.

"Now," the man said. "You."

He gave my wrist a quick twist. I screamed. My face was tear-soaked. Turns out, I couldn't stop them after all.

He let go of my arm. I just stood there, same as Mateo had, hunched over, head down, touching my wrist with my other hand. I tried to rub it, but stopped. The skin was bruised purple. I tried bending the wrist. Jesus.

A car drove past us. The woman in the passenger seat turned her head, staring. But they didn't stop, just kept going past the corner and down the next block.

I lowered my head again, stared straight down at my feet. I thought about telling the man I was sorry, but it didn't seem like it would help.

And anyway, I wasn't sorry. I needed that money more than this guy did. More than anybody.

Except I for sure didn't want my jaw broken or my teeth knocked out. So I had to at least try.

I raised my chin a couple of inches. Raised my eyes. "I'm sorry," I muttered.

"You're what?"

"Sorry," I said, louder.

He just kept watching me.

"Are you—" I swallowed, cleared my throat. It felt dry and thick, like someone had stuffed an old, wadded-up t-shirt down my mouth. "Are you going to call that other guy?"

He stared at me hard, probably another ten or fifteen seconds. My heart ticked off each second, jumping in my chest, in my throat, in my wrist.

Then he smiled. His smile oozed wide. "No. I think not. At least, not at the moment."

Air gushed up from my lungs. I guess I'd been holding my breath, waiting for him to answer.

"I do understand the allure of money," he said. "Which I presume was the motivation for your little venture into falsehood?" He raised his eyebrows at me. They were as thin as the hair on his scalp and the same pale color. It was a color I couldn't even name exactly, but it made me think of jellyfish. Something so thin and light that you could almost see through it.

I nodded, kind of confused. Of course it was the money. What else?

"I also appreciate initiative although you seem a bit low on cunning. You'll need to exercise your brain more stringently if you hope to achieve anything of true import."

Was that a compliment? I wasn't sure.

"However." He held up a finger. I stared at it. Fat, white, bulging like the skin wanted to split open at the knuckle. "However, you've wasted a considerable portion of my day. My time is valuable, young man. You've no idea how valuable."

He put his finger away. So then I just stared at his face, the lower part of it, the wobbly chins and the mouth.

I sucked in a big breath, swallowed down my heart. Made myself ask, "So . . . do I get any money?"

That mouth slid wider across his face. His fat neck shivered. It made me think of those blobs of yellow fat that hang off the end of a piece of raw chicken. He laughed. That should have made me feel relieved, but it didn't. My heart jumped all around between my stomach and the back of my mouth. I wondered what it was like to eat a bologna sandwich when you didn't have any teeth. Popsicles would still be easy. Jolly ranchers too.

"It's just that I really, really need it," I told him. "Not for dumb stuff, you know—" I flapped one of my hands. "Toys or candy. It's for something important."

"Is it now?" He sounded—well, not so mean. Nice? Not exactly. But like maybe he believed me. Like maybe he wouldn't mind helping. I let my gaze go a little higher, wanting to see his eyes.

But he'd turned to one side to check the comm he'd pulled out of his pocket. "Hmm," he said, I guess to himself. "Yes." I waited while he poked at the comm for at least five minutes, maybe longer.

When he put the comm away and looked at me again, I felt a little sick. He wasn't smiling now and his eyes were like bits of crushed ice.

"You'll want it in cash, I suppose?" he said.

I just stared. He was going to give me the money? Just like that? I should have been happy, right? But those eyes . . .

"I might see my way to slip you—say, two hundred?"

Two hundred! When we hadn't really seen Mr. Jennings' daughter? They'd have to take me at the emerald city if I showed up with two hundred dollars!

"Provided—" The man raised that finger again. "Provided that you assist me with a small matter. A trifle. I'm sure you won't mind. I expect you'd prefer to perform some useful task to earn such emolument rather than secure the sum by acting as a parasite."

I hated the way he talked. It was like he didn't really want me to understand. But I understood what he'd said about assisting. And I for sure understood about two hundred dollars.

"Okay," I said. "What d'you want me to do?"

"What is your experience," he said, raising that finger again, "with incendiary devices?"

"With what?"

"No mind." He wobbled over to his car and opened the back door. "Come on, boy. Hop in."

I edged closer and peered inside. That back seat was wide and covered with red velvet. It smelled so clean. The mats on the floor were cream-colored and they didn't have a speck on them. I was sweaty, streaks of dirt on my legs and my hair half-wet. My shoes were grimy and the laces black with old dried mud.

I glanced down the street at my house. My stomach felt all light and floaty. Never get in a car with a stranger. All the kids knew better than that.

But it wasn't my house. It was my mom's house. And officially Caveman Number Three's after tomorrow morning.

I yelled at myself inside my head. Are you serious about getting to the emerald city, Patros? Yeah? Then get your ass in the car!

I pitched myself onto the seat. Landed hard on my butt. It didn't matter because the velvet was cushiony and soft. I wallowed around in it. The man shut the door after me, got into the front, and started the engine. The engine was so smooth—or maybe the glass was so thick—that I could hardly hear it. Weird. There was glass between me and the front seat. What was that about? Maybe this guy didn't like to talk to anybody while he was driving around?

Which was okay by me. I couldn't understand most of what he said anyway.

Then music started playing. Piano, that old-fashioned classical-type stuff where it's just the music and nobody sings. It came from all around me, like it was floating out of the doors and the ceiling and the velvet seats. Not any song I'd ever heard before.

The car moved forward. The tires crunched over the chewed-up pavement and the car bounced softly up and down. I sat forward, my back stiff. Mr. Jennings' house was sliding away on one side of us and Mateo's house on the other. Mateo stared out from behind the screen door. Even from where I sat in the car, his eyes looked huge, like he couldn't believe what he saw.

I raised my hand, gave him a wave, letting him know I'd be okay, that I'd be back later with the money and say goodbye before I headed to the no-go. But he just kept staring, his head turning as we passed by. No wave, no smile, no thumbs up. Then I remembered the tinted glass and how dark it looked from the outside even though, from in here, I could see everything just fine.

He couldn't see me. Like the car had swallowed me and I was just . . . gone.

My heart did this weird sideways jerk, hard. There was a weird buzzing feeling all through my body, like my blood had turned into cherry Coke. I hitched my butt halfway up off the seat and twisted around to look back at Mateo. He'd come out onto his porch now that the car was past, but he kept staring after us. I had a crazy thought that maybe I should push the door open and jump out. Do it now while the car was moving slow.

But I just hunched there, blood buzzing in my head, and then the car turned left at the corner and picked up speed.

∞

I'm not sure how far we drove. It was maybe only fifteen or twenty minutes, but it seemed like forever. I leaned back again, but my whole body felt like a piece of wood, like something that couldn't bend. My hands were sweaty and I wiped them on the velvet. Made dark red streaks on it.

I've lived in Philly since I was born, but I guess I haven't actually been very far. Because it didn't take long before I didn't know where we were anymore. We weren't driving very fast and all the streets we went down looked pretty much like my own. Small houses, row houses, everything kind of falling apart and the car swerving around holes in the pavement. I wanted to ask the man how to get back to my street—just in case he for some reason didn't drive me all the way back home after we were done—but all I could see was the back of his head through the glass.

Then we slowed way down. The block we stopped on was short. There were houses on both sides, most of them abandoned-looking, with smashed-out windows, porch railings falling over, boards nailed over doors.

The engine shut off and Mr. Whelk pushed himself out of his seat. He came back and swung my door open. I looked past him, over his big shoulders and his head. The sun was going down behind the houses on that side of the street and the sky was a mess of orange and red. I had no idea what he could want me to do worth him paying me two hundred dollars. Unless he told me to sling some peel or synth on the wrong guy's turf? I'd seen what happened to people doing that kind of stuff. It was bad.

But then I saw something else over Mr. Whelk's shoulder and through a gap between a couple of the houses behind him. The no-go fence, metal shining red in the sunset. I knew the zone was big, but it still surprised me to think that fence ran all the way from my neighborhood down to this place. Seeing it there made me feel . . . I don't know, safer. Like I wasn't in such a strange place so far from home after all.

And seeing it reminded me what was wrong with home and why I needed the money. Even if I had to run synth, even if somebody took a shot at me doing it? Yeah. It was worth it.

I climbed out of the car.

"Excellent," Mr. Whelk said, but he was looking at one of the houses—number 415, the numbers spray-painted above the door—and not at me.

If my own house looked like shit, this place was like a whole sewer. It was two-stories and a dirty color somewhere between green and yellow. The porch roof had collapsed on one side. Sheets covered all the windows. The next four or five houses in either direction were completely boarded up.

I had that fizzy Coke feeling in my arms and legs again, and bubbling up in my chest. I just wanted to get this over with.

"Mr. Whelk?" I said.

He held a hand up like he wanted me to stop talking. I thought about how hard that hand gripped around my wrist. I shut up.

He looked up and down the street, looked across the street, checked the whole block. Like I said, it was short, not too many houses, and most of those were wrecks. I didn't see a single person anywhere.

"Very nice." Mr. Whelk went around to the trunk. He popped it and disappeared behind the raised lid. He closed it quietly and limped back to me. He carried two metal containers. He held one up for me to see.

It looked kind of like a large metal bottle. Like something you'd pour milk into to keep it cold all day. All I could think was that he'd filled it with synth caps or some other kind of drug.

He nestled the bottle against his belly and waved a hand at the house. "You see before you number four fifteen."

He waited, like I was supposed to say something. "Okay," I answered.

"This is the structure in need of your attention."

"My . . . why?"

A smile slid across his fat cheeks. He laughed and all his chins flopped up and down. "Yours is not to question why. Yours is to—" He laughed again. I had no idea what he thought was so funny, but just hearing him laugh sent another burst of that sick, fizzy feeling through me. He pushed the metal bottles into my arms. "Well, let's just say the owners of this atrocity at four-fifteen have been involved in some nefarious business. The entire structure is in need of a good scouring."

I blinked at the bottles. I blinked at Mr. Whelk. "Scouring?" I know I sounded like a stupid little kid, like the twins. Did the metal bottles have water in them? Soap? "Do I need a sponge?" I asked.

Mr. Whelk shook his head at me. "Water is insufficient for the degree of purification required in this instance." He took a step back and gave me a little nod.

I just stood there, clutching the containers. What did he want me to do? Go in the house and clean it somehow? But that didn't make any sense.

"Let's be generous and blame a grievously flawed public school system for your incomprehension," he said, "rather than congenital doltishness." I didn't move. He sighed. "There are things inside this house that are dangerous. That need to be destroyed themselves before they further infest our fair city."

"Things? What—"

"The exact nature of the items is on a need-to-know basis. But I assure you, you'll be doing a good work here today. Now. All you do is—"

"I don't get it."

"You don't need to 'get it'. You only need to—"

"I want to underst—"

"Goddamnit! You don't need to understand anything." Mr. Whelk leaned over me. He was a giant. I cringed down, sure he was about to bust me with one huge fist. His face was a spotty purple, even his chins, like one of those big thunderhead clouds that looms up right before the rain cracks down. "You just need to do as you're told, boy. Unless you've changed your mind and you'd prefer to meet my coworker."

The bone-breaker? "No, that's okay."

Mr. Whelk bent down, glared right into my eyes. "Wise decision. Your jaw thanks you." He shook his arms and shoulders as he stood up straight again. The thundercloud moved on. He was smiling again. I needed to pee. Being nervous—okay, scared—does that to me.

"You take those." He flicked a look at the metal bottles. Now he talked very slow and plain, like he wanted to make sure I understood. "Take them into the house, the first floor. Go to the back door. Take the first device, pull this back." He tapped at a small metal ring near the top, pretended to pull at it. "You'll hear a snapping sound. Keep pulling until the ring goes completely flat against the side here. Then set the device on the floor, just inside the back door. Go to the front door. Do the same thing with the second device. Then exit the house. Preferably at speed."

"What?"

Mr. Whelk sighed again. "Fast. Leave fast, through the front door."

"What if somebody sees me? Is anybody in there?"

"You don't need to worry about that."

"But what if?"

"If you should happen to see anyone inside the house, they won't bother you. They won't even realize you're there."

"So there are people."

"Along with the roaches and rodents, yes. I expect there are."

I rubbed one of the metal containers with a fingertip. "Will they get hurt?"

"Not to worry. These will get rid of all the pests."

I shot a look at the house. Nothing had changed. Nothing moved, but who could tell what was going on behind the boards, behind the green sheets? What he was saying gave me a weird feeling. Spooky. Like I was going to turn into a ghost as soon as I went in there. "But how do you know?" I said.

"Trust me, I know."

Then Mr. Whelk was counting out money and pressing it into my hand.

"One hundred," he said. The way his voice dropped down, it was like he said, "The end."

I rubbed my fingers over the bills. I loved that thick, smooth feel of the paper. I was afraid to complain about the amount. One hundred was a lot more than I'd ever had in my life. But . . . it wasn't what he'd promised. I looked up at Mr. Whelk. "You—I mean, I thought you said two hundred."

"Half now, half when the job's done. That's how business works. I won't even charge you for the lesson." Mr. Whelk leaned against the hood of his car. It sank and let out a small, squashed groan. He tapped the billfold he still held in one hand, crossed his arms, and lifted his eyebrows at me.

For a second, I thought about taking the hundred and running into the zone now. But I wanted to say goodbye to Mateo. And I wanted one last look at my mom before I left for good. Don't ask me why.

I headed toward the house.

The front yard was about the size of a bathtub. It was all dirt and trash. I waded through crumpled soda cans and potato chip bags. The yard smelled like rotting food and dog pee.

Climbing up onto the porch felt like going into a cave. There were rusty old bicycle parts piled back in the shadows and a heap of old car batteries leaking black gunk onto the boards. Wasp nests stuck like paper pineapples in all the corners of the roof, with one right above the front door. Wasps buzzed away from the porch and came shooting back, fast.

That hurried me up. The faster I got past the nests, the less chance I'd get stung. So I scrunched my head down and pushed through the front door.

God, it stank. I smelled the room before I'd even made it all the way inside. I stopped just past the doorway and put my free hand over my mouth and nose and squinted through the shadows.

I was standing in a living room, I guess you'd call it. There was a couch anyway, and a coffee table. I felt like I was down at the bottom of a dirty old fish tank. The room was nothing but moldy green light coming through the sheets over the windows and sliming its way down the stairs from the second floor. It smelled like mushrooms, a dark, wet stink.

Plastic trashbags covered the floor. They looked like giant beetles, humped up in the dark. Some of them had split open, leaking out dirty clothes, crumpled-up kleenexes. The trash rippled in the shadows. It took me a minute to realize that roaches skittered over the garbage. I looked up. Black dots scuttled over the ceiling.

I'm not scared of bugs, but this was beyond gross.

I could hardly believe anybody lived in this place, but Mr. Whelk sure had made it sound like people did.

It made my skin go prickly and my face feel tight when I thought about whether anybody else was in here with me. I swung my head to look at the stairs.

Empty.

The couch.

Empty, I think, but it was hard to tell for certain with the trashbags mountained on one end and blankets on the other.

The faster I got this done, the better.

I tucked my head down and headed toward the doorway to the next room. It was hard keeping my balance. The plastic bags were lumpy and loose. They slithered under my sneakers. I imagined how that next hundred dollars would feel in my hand. How it would feel when I was living in the emerald city, floating on my back in that pool way up in the air.

Just had to get through this first.

The next room was also the last. It was brighter than the living room, orange sunset pushing in through a raggedy screen door at the back and ripping itself up on the smashed window glass. There was a table covered with papers and one wooden chair.

There was also a person—all wrapped up from head to foot in a dirty gray sheet—sitting on the chair.

I stopped dead and stared, not even breathing, my heart cutting out my ribs.

The person in the sheet didn't make any sound. Were they dead? Propped up some way in the chair? I felt like I was about to bust out of my skin, I wanted to get out of there so bad.

A trash heap covered this floor too. I put my feet down careful and slow, trying not to make any noise. Which was impossible, of course. I cringed every time my sneakers crushed down on a wrapper or rustled through the paper.

But the person on the chair still didn't move. I edged in a careful circle, moving around them, keeping as far away as I could, but wanting to see, wanting to know for sure. The sheet made a hood covering the person's hair and head, everything except the face. It came slowly into view as I moved forward.

My pulse jumped higher. It was a woman. And she wasn't dead.

She stared straight across at an empty cabinet with its door ripped off. Her face was gray, like the sheet.

Her mouth was too. Her eyes didn't move, barely even blinked. She had sores, pink and runny, on her forehead and a blank look in her face like she was staring at something inside her own head.

I'd seen enough peelfreaks around my neighborhood to know she was one. I let out my breath. Okay, just a peelfreak, just a druggy skinwaste. It was a relief, in a way, because she wasn't going to bother me, or even notice I was in her house. But it still gave me that sick, cold feeling. Like I was seeing a ghost, something dead. Or maybe more like I was the ghost.

I hurried past her and set one of the metal containers Mr. Whelk had given me next to the door. Mr. Whelk was right that this place was full of pests and they needed to be killed. But what exactly was this thing going to do? Send poison floating through the house?

For a second I hesitated. But the bug-killing companies probably made poisons that only killed the cockroaches and silverfish and left the people alone.

I thought about the feel of the money against my fingers and I pulled the ring.

I had to yank hard, but then it gave all of the sudden and clicked into place just like Mr. Whelk said it would. I crouched there for a second, watching and listening, but nothing happened. Ivy on the back window scratched against the glass.

Then I remembered what else Mr. Whelk had said. About being fast.

Why had he said that? Because the poison would wake up the people and they'd come after me for breaking into their house?

I held the other container close against my stomach and slipped and stumbled back into the living room. A bag fell off the couch. Something heaved up from underneath the pile. Another person. Man, woman, I couldn't tell. The room was too dark and they were still half-buried under mildewed blankets.

This one didn't say anything either, but turned its head, following me as I slopped my way running across the floor and skidded onto my knees by the door. Behind me, another bag rustled and dropped from the couch onto the floor. I looked back. A face made of bone, eyes like gray swamps, staring right at me, stick arms trying to push the body up onto its feet.

I shoved Mr. Whelk's device onto the floor and ripped the ring straight back.

Then I ran, straight out the door. I forgot about the wasp nest and I wasn't two steps onto the porch before I got stung twice, on my right arm and the side of my neck. It hurt like hell, like needles sliding under the skin.

I yelped and bolted across the yard to the street where Mr. Whelk leaned against his car and laughed. All his chins laughed with him. Sweat glittered red on his face and throat.

"Hey!" I said. "You said nobody would even know I was in there. But there's a guy—I mean, a girl—a—"

He wasn't looking at me. He was looking past me and laughing this soft low sort of chuckle, way deep in his throat. I spun half-around to see what was so funny.

The windows had turned into fire. The sheets over them burned white-orange, crumbling and smoking around the edges. Wasps flew out of the nests. A rat crawled out of the garbage in the yard and headed across the street. I just stood there, staring at the shut door, ice water freezing in my gut.

Mr. Whelk's hand—heavy, like a chunk of metal—landed on my shoulder and pinched me down to the bone. Tears shot into my eyes.

"Well done," he said, his voice very smooth, very calm. "No pun intended."

What? I struggled out of his grip. "There's people in there."

"*Exactement.*"

I had to make him understand. "You didn't say there'd be fire." I grabbed at his arm, tried to pull him toward the house. But I couldn't drag him, couldn't even budge him an inch.

"Actually, I did. Blame your anemic vocabulary." He shook my hand loose.

The house simmered. I darted forward into the yard, but I kept looking back at Mr. Whelk, waving at him, trying to get him to help me. A wall of heat pressed out from the house, pushing me away.

Mr. Whelk stepped up beside me. For a second, I thought he was coming to help me. He reached into a pocket and brought something out. He gripped my hand and I felt the bills, cool and creamy, against my palm.

He dropped my hand and stepped back. His eyes were red and flickering, reflecting the flames cracking through the front door and the bloody egg of sunset sliding behind the roof. "There's no need to feel bad about the house or any of its contents in the process of—ahh—being purged. Trust me, none of the—hmm—items currently ablaze deserve an instant of your pity. However—" A smile sweated onto his mouth. His lips shone like he'd oiled them. "There is the slight difficulty that officially, from this point forward, you'll be considered a murderer."

My whole body burst into fever. Murderer? That couldn't be right. Nobody would believe—but one glance at those sheets shriveling to black around the windows and I realized that, yes, everybody would believe it. Because it would be true.

"I wouldn't advise you to discuss this little incident with the police," Mr. Whelk said. "Penitentiaries are so unpleasant these days. Even the juvenile variety. Of course, you could spend the rest of your life in hiding."

I thought of the sheet inside the house, the one wrapped around the woman in the kitchen. Wrapping her up in fire. Unless she'd gone out the back door?

I started for the side of the house, but Mr. Whelk grabbed the back of my shirt and dragged me back to him. "You'll find I've paid you in full. Next time, you might think twice before you send a false alert to any of my men." He made a sound in his throat that was dark and rough like a crow. Like one of my mom's cavemen right after he'd punched me in the back or slapped me hard across the face. Pleased with himself.

Then Mr. Whelk dropped me and flapped his fingers out, shooing me off and turning toward his car as he spoke. "In the meantime, it might be best for you to vacate the—"

But I was already off, shooting around the side of the house, my legs ripping through the heat. The weeds went flat under my feet. I slid through more trash, almost falling, catching myself with one hand that sank into a gooey stew of rotting garbage.

Then I was around the house and at the back. I couldn't go up on the porch. I tried, but the heat pushed me back. I flung myself from side to side, stretching my neck, trying to see through the door or the broken-out window.

The window was a square of fire. Flames snapped through the screen door and crackled through the wooden frame. She couldn't be alive in there. Nobody could be. Could they?

I had to know. I kept plunging in toward the door, then dodging back out again. Nothing but fire in my eyes.

Then—I could hardly believe it. The screen door shifted, just an inch or two, the dead-black metal swinging slightly out. I stopped where I was and stared. My heart was climbing up my tongue. If she was alive and Mr. Whelk was wrong and I wasn't a murderer—I could go home and maybe the caveman would even be gone. Everything could still be okay. I wanted my mom. I wanted the emerald city but I wanted my mom too. I don't even know why.

The door opened and opened. Fire swam in it, swam in the kitchen, rose up from the floor and dripped from the ceiling.

The woman was on her feet, stopped just inside the door. She still had the sheet pulled tight around her, but it was on fire too. She took a step into the open doorway. Fire burned straight up off of her, like a torch. Her hair popped and crackled. Another step. Her face was calm, her eyes still staring into her own head. She didn't even know she was on fire.

I wanted to yell at her to get out here, get down on the ground, roll around in the dirt and the trash. But it was like my throat was full of dirt, and my heart and my veins were stuffed full, too, and all I could do was watch when she took one more step, wobbled, and then collapsed backward into the flames.

I shuffled forward and back. I couldn't decide which way to go. My hair was dripping, my face was soaked and I didn't know if it was from sweat or from crying.

I reached up to rub at my eyes and something fell from my hand. I looked down, following it. Five twenty-dollar bills flew toward the fire at the back door like it was sucking them in on its breath. The paper flared up and sank out of sight. The fire ate every ashy bit.

I stumbled back to the alley. Dug into my pocket, felt the other hundred dollars folded there.

My mom was a hundred miles away. So was my house and Mateo and the twins. Even Cave Man Number Three was there. With the people who hadn't killed other people.

The sun was almost down. The fence to the no-go zone was black against the darkening sky. It reared up over me, tall as a dinosaur, the razor wire at the top like teeth. I gripped the metal, pushed my face against it, smelled the rust and the dirt. I held the wire and I shivered like the thing was electrified. It wasn't supposed to happen like this.

What if they were right? The grown-ups, the people who said there wasn't an emerald city? What if it was just trashed buildings, smashed cars, skinwaste runaways chasing each other with guns and knives through the streets?

But that couldn't be true. Because that meant there was nowhere for me. And there had to be some place. *Had* to be.

I unfolded my fingers, stepped back, got my breath back. Got *myself* back.

The emerald city would be there. I believed in it. I would *make* myself believe in it. And it wouldn't be long now. Maybe even by morning, I'd be there, up at the top of the castle, floating in the blue water, staring up at the clouds, cleaning myself in the sky. A hundred dollars would be enough.

I headed left along the fence, looking for a slice in the wire, looking for a way in.

If you enjoyed these stories, be sure to read the companion novel, **Executables**, available in electronic and print from your favorite online retailers.

About the Authors

Lisa Cindrich is the author of the children's historical novel, **In the Shadow of the Pali**, which was a selection of both the Junior Library Guild and the New York Public Library's Books for the Teen Age, as well as **Executables**, a dystopian thriller. She currently lives in the Kansas City area (on the Kansas side.)

Jay Sparks' debut novel was **Executables**. He also resides in the Kansas City metro area (on the Missouri side.)

Visit the authors at unmooredpress.com or shoot them an email at unmooredpress@gmail.com.

If you'd like to find out about releases and giveaways as soon as they become available, subscribe to Unmoored Press' electronic newsletter, available via the website.